Mountain Laurel

by

Donna Fasano

First edition 2011

Second edition 2013
ISBN-10: 1939000211
ISBN-13: 978-1-939000-21-7

Cover Design: Najla Qamber Designs

Chapter One

"This is just great!" Laurel slapped her hand against the steering wheel. "First I leave my wallet at that two-bit, sorry excuse for a diner. Then we get lost. And now I've got to change a flat tire." The car lurched forward slowly as she scanned the road ahead for a wide enough embankment so she could pull over.

"Who said kidnapping would be easy?"

The sullen teen's words grated on her already frayed nerves. "Ginny." Laurel's jaw was so tight she felt the beginnings of a tension headache shooting up her neck and into her skull. "There is no law against protecting someone you love."

"Oh! So that's what you're doing." Ginny's acerbic tone continued as she placed a hand on her chest and feigned a dramatic apology. "Forgive me. *Please*. I thought taking a person off to God knows where without her permission was called abduction."

Rather than feeling guilty, as Ginny clearly wanted, to her surprise, Laurel's aggravation vanished as quickly as it had erupted. The rigidity in her upper body eased and she relaxed against the seat, a mischievous grin tipping one corner of her mouth. "Oh, but little sister, I had your permission. It's not my fault that you were inebriated to the point of waking with a gap in your memory."

"I wasn't drunk."

Laurel glanced over just as lines of angry denial furrowed Ginny's brow. Compressed lips and tightly crossed arms completed the look of defiance that had become all too familiar lately. Arguing was useless. Her sister's wild, destructive behavior left Laurel feeling hopelessly bewildered. What could she possibly do to help Ginny? Nothing. Nothing, that is, until Ginny herself realized what a dangerous path she was racing down. The same deadly path their brother had followed.

She had suppressed her suspicions for months, refusing to believe that Ginny would experiment with drugs or alcohol. Especially since Ginny knew those were the very things that had caused their brother's tragic and untimely death.

Her grip on the steering wheel tightened. *I won't stand still and watch Ginny kill herself*, Laurel silently argued. *I may have been too young to help Brian, but I will help Ginny. I will! No matter what I have to do.*

"Where are we, anyway?"

Her sister's strained voice pulled Laurel from her thoughts just in time for her to spot a wide area on the side of the road and pull onto it. "We're on vacation," she replied, shoving the gear stick into park and shutting off the engine.

Ginny gave a disgruntled sniff. "Does Dad know about this '*vacation*'?"

"Yes, and we have his blessing." Laurel was happy to answer Ginny's questions since this was the first sign of interest, hostile or otherwise, she had shown in the trip.

"And he's actually going to stay home and care for Mom?"

"Uh-huh." Laurel hoped her voice didn't betray the uncertainty she felt over their father's trustworthiness. She had plenty of doubts about him actually following through on his promise. But sometimes, problems had to be prioritized.

"Amazing!" Ginny remarked. "And exactly where is this vacation taking us? It looks like the middle of nowhere."

"You're about to enter the town of Oakland, set in the scenic mountains of western Maryland. Rest and relax as you watch wild creatures frolic in the lush, tranquil forest."

Ginny's mouth cracked into the smallest of grins. "You sound like a brochure put out by the tourist council."

"A smile." Laurel's voice filled with warmth. "That's what I wanted to see." Reaching out and taking her sister's hand, she waited until their gazes met and then softly added, "We'll have a good time, Ginny. You'll see."

She ignored the skeptical look her sister shot her and glanced out at the tree-covered mountains, the autumn colors swirling in vibrant harmony.

"You have to admit it's a beautiful place," Laurel said. "It was nice of Jim to loan us his house for a couple of weeks."

"So—" Ginny nodded knowingly "—this is Jim's fault. I knew Dad shouldn't have hired him."

"Ginny!" Laurel chuckled as she freed the keys from the ignition. "He's a great guy. You're just angry because he's not interested in you."

"Yeah, well, don't you find that a little strange?" Ginny's eyes narrowed. "I mean, I could have a date seven nights a week if I wanted. I sometimes do. Why won't he take me out?"

Laurel lifted her shoulders in a tiny shrug. "He's been busy working in the store, plus he's been working on fixing up the upstairs apartment."

"That's weird, too." Ginny slid around and bent her knee up onto the seat. "Have you been up there? He sure is meticulous about how he wants things." Her eyes lit up as an idea hit her. "Do you think he's gay?"

Laurel laughed outright and shook her head. "That kind of stereotyping is rude, little sister. A man can be neat and organized, *and not be attracted to you*, and still be heterosexual."

"Well..." Ginny sounded unconvinced. "I still think it's weird." Unlatching her seat belt, she gave Laurel a curious look. "If he's moving to Ocean City, what do you think he'll do with his house here?"

"It doesn't belong to him." Laurel unfastened her own seat belt. "He rents from an uncle or something."

"Does this 'uncle or something' know we're coming?"

"He should," Laurel said. "Jim said he'd call. But we won't be going anywhere until we get this flat tire changed."

"Don't look at me," Ginny whined. "I didn't even want to come on this trip."

"Get out of the car and help me with this. It's going to be fun." Laurel slammed the door.

"Sure," Ginny muttered, shoving open her door and stepping onto the gravel shoulder of the road. "Let's have us some *fun*."

~ ~ ~

Michael had never been hungrier in his life. Then again, he remembered ruefully, he always felt like this after a three-day survival trek. He rubbed a hand over his growling stomach. Knowing you could survive in the mountains on wild berries, Indian cucumbers and sassafras tea was all well and good, but right now all he could think about was the thick, juicy steak waiting for him in the freezer.

Rounding a sharp bend in the road, he saw a young girl sitting on a pile of luggage next to a dusty brown sedan. As he pulled onto the scenic overlook, she stood and waved. He frowned. That steak would have to wait.

Michael got out of his truck. "You having trouble?" He rolled up his sleeves, hoping this wouldn't take long.

"Just a flat tire." She flashed a come-hither smile. "We almost have it fixed." She brushed a long strand of silky blond hair over her shoulder.

He watched with amusement as she strutted toward him, and he knew all that was missing from the well- practiced teenage production was a slight batting of the eyes. Knowing when he was being flirted with, Michael was flattered, but then, he also knew teenage girls weren't particular on whom they practiced.

"We?" he questioned.

Just then a head popped up from behind the car. The setting sun reflected like fire off the jumble of shimmering copper curls. Emerald eyes gazed at him from a beautiful face streaked with grease and grime.

He became uncomfortable as those green eyes narrowed, scrutinizing every detail of his person. She glanced past him to inspect his truck, and when her gaze returned to his face, it was dark with suspicion.

"Need some help?" He did his best to soften the edge of irritation he heard in his voice. It wasn't her fault he was starving.

"Thanks, but I'm almost finished." Her brow was pinched, her whole body tense as she rose to a stand.

Her reaction made him pause and think about what he looked like; unshaven, mud-spattered, bedraggled. Hell, he looked little better than a homeless derelict. Why wouldn't she be wary?

Absently running a hand over his whiskered jaw, he tried to explain. "This is what three days roughing it in—"

He'd taken a step toward her wearing what he thought was a friendly expression, but seeing her grip tighten on the tire iron, he stopped short and swallowed hard.

The younger girl sidled up beside him, oblivious to the apprehension her companion was feeling.

"I'm glad you're here," the teen said.

Her silky hair brushed against his skin as she placed a hand on his arm. "You can check out my sister's handiwork. I'd hate to have that tire fall off while we're driving down the road."

Her laughter was cut short by the burning glare she received from the fiery-haired amateur mechanic.

"I'm finished, Ginny. Let's go."

"But you're missing one of those nut things."

Listening to this exchange, Michael moved around to have a look at the tire. Sure enough, one wheel stud was bare. He was about to advise these women that driving with a missing lug nut wasn't safe, but before he could, the woman clutching the metal rod spoke.

"It'll be fine. We're going. Get into the car. Now."

"I don't think so," Michael said quietly.

"I beg your pardon?"

The impact of her anger took him by surprise when she directed the full force of it at him. He realized her fear, but seeing that they drove away safely outweighed it. Besides, her alarm was unfounded. She'd learn that soon enough, if she gave him half a chance.

"I think we should look around for the lug nut," he told her. "It couldn't have rolled far." He stepped away from the teenager, who had crouched down to look under the car.

"There, Laurel!" she exclaimed, pointing. "It's right there. See? This guy's cute *and* he's right."

"Laurel." The name rolled off Michael's tongue

9

in a whisper too low for anyone to hear. What a beautiful name. It fit her perfectly.

He watched her crouch down and reach under the car, his gaze sliding down the graceful curve of her spine, over shapely hips, settling on the firm corduroy-clad bottom covered with sand and grit.

Tearing his gaze away, he found himself looking directly into the lively eyes of the younger girl. The knowing smile on the flirtatious teen's face said a mouthful, and Michael couldn't help grinning with her in acceptance of being caught.

Laurel tightened the last lug nut as quickly as she could, unaware of the silent conspiracy taking place over her head. She would have been quite satisfied with her job had it not been for the man who had suddenly shown up to "help." Quickly checking out the stranger once more, she found him sharing a smile with Ginny. Anger overrode her distrust. Their silent conversation was clearly unwholesome, and she was furious that this man would leer at her sister. And the way her chin was dipped, Ginny seemed to be egging him on!

Using every ounce of her ire, Laurel cranked the jack like there was no tomorrow and soon had all four tires on the ground. Holding tight to the cold steel of the tire iron, she dragged the jack from under the car with her free hand and straightened.

"Excuse me," she snapped as she stepped between them on her way to dump the jack into the trunk. Returning for the flat tire, she none too politely refused the man's offer to help.

"If you help her," Ginny jeered, "she won't be

able to hold this over my head. And believe me, she will!"

Prickling, Laurel watched the laughing dark eyes of the man as he shared the joke with Ginny. In her haste to leave, she had put the jack in lopsided, which kept the tire from sitting properly. Frustrated, she pounded on the false bottom that covered the tire, trying to get it to lie flat. Whirling around, Laurel snapped at Ginny, "You'll have to reload the suitcases. My hands are filthy."

"Now I, unlike my dear sister, would never turn down an offer of help."

The teen's eyes glittered as she spoke to Michael, and he was relieved to finally get a chance to assist. He'd had to stuff his hands deep into his pockets to squelch the urge to interfere when the improperly placed jack had caused so much trouble. But instinct had told him standing back would be wiser than possibly being thumped on the head with a tire iron.

Laurel moved out of the way and watched her sister and the stranger pack the cases into the trunk. She noticed the man carefully arrange them around the off-kilter false bottom and felt heat rise up her neck to scorch her cheeks. Maybe she had been silly for being afraid. It was obvious he wanted to help. She watched his dark eyes dance and sparkle with humor. Now that her fear had abated a bit, the joking and laughter he shared with Ginny seemed warm and genuine, and Laurel liked the sound of it. He did need a shave, but she liked the way the sun glinted off his sleek brown hair, and the way the muscles of his tanned forearms rippled as he lifted the...

What was she thinking? Laurel blinked, mentally shaking herself. The guy could be an ax murderer for all she knew, and she was standing here admiring his muscles! She started when he slammed the trunk's lid, his gaze suddenly connecting with hers. The conflicting emotions warring inside her caused another rush of heat to flush her face and neck.

"Would you mind if I made a suggestion?" he asked.

"Of course not," she replied grudgingly.

"There's a service station about fifteen miles up the road. I think you should stop and have the attendant check the tire. He'll tighten the lug nuts with air compression and he might be able to plug the flat."

"Thanks, but we won't be going that far." Laurel was pleased with her flippancy and motioned their departure to Ginny with a jerk of her head. She spun around and walked along the side of the car. The man's stare on her back caused a tingling sensation to travel up her spine.

"One more suggestion?"

His quiet voice forced her to turn once again in his direction. Laurel flashed him a mockingly patient look and waited.

"Dust off your bottom before you get in."

Ginny giggled before disappearing into the car and slamming her door shut. Laurel fixed him with a burning glare of disgust before pulling open her own door and slipping into her seat, and it took every bit of willpower she possessed not to brush off her rear before doing so.

"I don't think it's all that funny," Laurel growled at her sister. Her scowl deepened as she caught sight of the man in the rear-view mirror still wearing that irritating grin.

Michael shook his head as he watched the car drive away. He shouldn't have teased her, but he'd become aggravated knowing she would probably let her pride get in the way of her safety. He knew she would pass the gas station and hoped she had sense enough to stop. She must have a lousy sense of direction and distance, because the only thing between the overlook and the station was the cabin he rented to his cousin Jim.

~ ~ ~

Steam filled the tiny bathroom as hot water beat down on Laurel's back. The steady spray slowly washed away her tension. She was sorry for yelling at Ginny while they were driving to the cabin. They hadn't been in the car two seconds after the tire incident before her tirade had started. The fatigue she'd felt was no excuse for the bitter words she'd spat at Ginny.

"I can't believe your behavior!" Laurel had barely contained the impulse to hit the steering wheel with the heel of her hand. "You're not a kid any more. You're almost eighteen years old. You should know better. That man could have been an escaped convict, a thief, a rapist! At best he was some dirty vagrant stopping with the hopes of getting a few bucks off two fluttery females."

Ginny had opened her mouth to protest, but whatever she'd been about to say had been crushed by Laurel's continued onslaught.

"Did you see that dilapidated truck?" Her eyebrows had shot up toward her hairline. "Did you notice the fact that there was a gun hanging in the back window?" Laurel had sucked in an angry breath. "Is it too much to ask for you to use a little common sense? Just a little!" That time she had hit the steering wheel with force enough to bruise her hand.

"Are you ever going to grow up?" Her words had been husky with exasperation. "Don't you know it's not safe to flirt with a complete stranger?"

Ginny had lifted her chin stubbornly. "I wasn't flirting. And it was you he was gawking at! Jeez, the man practically drooled!"

Laurel had been floored. And even though more than four hours had passed since their narrow escape, she was still stunned. The needles of steaming water didn't provide enough heat to stop Laurel's involuntary shiver as she thought of being ogled by that degenerate when her back was turned. They'd been lucky to get away from him unharmed. And to think she had admired him! Pushing the frightening thoughts from her mind, she lifted her face to the hot spray.

Think of pleasant things, she chided herself.

She sighed, shoving the ugliness from her mind. Then she remembered Ginny's dismay when they had driven up the narrow dirt lane on Spring Mountain to find that Jim's house was a small rustic cottage, and she smiled. Laurel's own trepidation had

14

vanished when she'd discovered that the tiny log cabin had all the comforts of home. Plus a few added attractions.

She grinned as she remembered the mouse that had sent Ginny into hysterics. Calming her had been a feat in itself. Finally, Laurel had clapped the car keys into her hand, gave her hasty directions and thrust her out the door with orders to bring a pizza home for dinner. She had promised Ginny the mouse would be gone before she returned. Catching it hadn't been easy.

Laurel considered spending another minute or two under the deliciously hot spray, then reluctantly turned the porcelain handle, knowing Ginny wouldn't appreciate having to take a cold shower. She pulled back the curtain, plucked a fluffy white towel off the bar and wrapped her hair, turban-style. Contentment spread through her relaxed muscles.

She knew that she'd done the right thing. Ginny was away from the hooligans she'd been running around with back home. The two of them had the opportunity to get close again, to talk. Laurel would make Ginny see the need to go to college and do something with her life.

The front door opened and closed. As Laurel tucked another towel around her body and secured it under her arm, she wondered how Ginny could have gotten back so quickly, then realized she must have forgotten to take money.

"Hey! You in there?" The loud rap on the bathroom door caused every muscle in Laurel's body to clench. But what chilled her blood was recognizing the deep male voice.

Chapter Two

Oh, God! It was him. He'd followed them. He must have lurked in the bushes until Ginny left. And now he's in the house!

Panic flooded through her body, through her brain, making it difficult to move, difficult to think. Her mouth felt dry as dust and she swallowed painfully. Through the haze of hysteria one thought streamed in her mind: lock the door! She pushed the button of the flimsy lock. The click echoed loudly in the utter stillness.

"Hey!" Excitement turned his voice insistent.

Turning, she scanned the room for a weapon. She wouldn't let him get her without a fight. Brush. Mirror. Mascara. Nothing heavy enough to hurt a man. Laurel had never been so frightened in her life. Frantically, she looked around the tiny bathroom. Her eyes lit on the window high above the toilet. Would it be possible? It was small, the type where the glass moved out and up as it was cranked open.

She quickly glanced down at her towel-clad body and decided she couldn't possibly escape stark naked! Seeing a discarded outfit that Ginny had wadded up and tossed into a corner, Laurel was grateful for her sister's usually infuriating habit of changing clothes three times a day. Laurel pulled the lime-green sweater over her head and, after pushing one arm through, noticed it was inside out. This is no time to be chic, she thought, shoving her other arm into the soft knitted material.

"Open up!"

Laurel's eyes darted to the door in time to see the knob jiggle violently. Thrusting one foot, then the other, into a pair of rumpled culottes, she had to suck in her breath and shimmy them over her hips. They were tight, but they'd work. She scooped up one crew sock and pulled it on, the sock's heel protruding awkwardly over her ankle. The two sharp raps that sounded against the door forced her to leave her other foot bare.

Not losing another second, she stood on the toilet seat lid, cranked open the window and punched out the screen. It would be a tight fit, but it was the only way out. Tiny bug carcasses crunched under her palms when she placed her hands on the sill, but she barely noticed. She pulled with all her might. The shiny pine paneling was slick and she slipped twice, both times her knee banged painfully into the wall. She squealed when, in her thrashing to get up to the window, her foot hit the hand mirror, sending it crashing to the floor.

"What the devil is going on in there? Open this door!" Angry bangs vibrated in the room.

Sweat broke out on her forehead and upper lip. Pulling with all her might, she hoisted herself up to the window. Tears of fear and frustration blurred her vision and her arms quivered from exertion. Her head and shoulders were through the opening, but she could no longer reach the porcelain tank with her feet, so she lost her leverage point. Shifting her torso one way, then the other, she inched further out the narrow window.

She heard a great weight crash against the bathroom door. *Oh, God, I'll never make it*, she thought, wriggling more desperately.

The second impact against the door caused the wood to splinter, and Laurel screamed with what little air was left in her lungs. When that was gone, she breathed as deeply as the tiny window opening would allow and screamed again.

After rubbing his shoulder, Michael hit the door a third time. It finally gave way and slammed against the wall.

He stepped into the bathroom, shards of glass crunching under his shoes. "What the hell..."

Seeing the half-clothed, definitely female body squirming half in and half out of the tiny bathroom window stopped him in his tracks. Her bloodcurdling screams made the hairs on the back of his neck stand on end. He stood for several seconds, stunned motionless. What the heck was he supposed to do?

The screeching finally ceased. He watched as the wiggling stopped and one satiny leg stretched down. The toes of the one bare foot were a scant two inches from reaching the toilet tank. He considered grasping the slim ankles and guiding them down but quickly rejected the notion to touch the intruder.

Michael turned and strode out of the bathroom and out of the front door. He rounded the corner of the house to where the body protruded from the window.

The woman's head was draped in a towel that covered her face. Reaching up, he snatched it off and was rewarded with another scream.

"Don't you touch me! Don't you come near me!" She furiously brushed at the wet hair plastered against her forehead and cheeks.

Michael's eyes widened. It was the woman from the car. Laurel. But what in the world was she doing here?

"I mean it!" She twisted, hitting her elbow against the heavy logs on the outside of the cabin. Her sharp intake of breath knocked him out of his shocked silence.

"Are you okay?" he asked.

"Don't you come near me!" Her voice sounded deadly intense.

"Look," he said, "you're obviously in trouble up there. Let me help you."

"You touch me," she threatened, glaring at him, "and you'll be the sorriest man to ever live."

"I don't know what you're thinking, but I'm not here to hurt you."

Laurel heard the words but didn't believe them. And then her brows knit together in confusion. He looked different.

"Let me help you down," he said.

"No! I mean it. I don't want your help." Her voice was weakening as she tried to put her finger on it. Decent, that was it. He looked decent—freshly shaved. And clean. But it was him all right. She'd never forget those dark eyes.

"Fine, that's fine. I'll stay right here." He held his hands up as though surrendering.

"I want you to go away. Right now." To her mortification, a single, fat tear welled in her eye and slid down her cheek.

"When you get down, we'll talk." He spoke with firm intent, his fists resting on his hips.

She was afraid. Probably more so than she'd ever been in her life. But pain began to flare around her ribcage, where the dead weight of her body pressed against the metal window frame.

"Please, just go away." The pleading in her voice angered her into a new resolve. "Now!"

"Get. Down." He put equal emphasis on both words.

"I can't!" she yelled. "I'm stuck!"

They glared at each other for several seconds.

Heaving a sigh, he said, "I'm coming in to help you."

She watched him stride out of sight, helpless to do anything but hang there. She felt like a snared rabbit. A snared rabbit wearing too tight shorts that were riding up her back side. Fighting down the panic that was rebuilding in her chest, she focused on his words of assistance and prayed he was being truthful. The powerlessness she felt was totally unnerving.

Back in the bathroom, Michael wondered what to do first. Those long shapely legs were distracting. After placing several towels over the broken glass on the floor, he reached up and planted his hands on her hips—and he was promptly rewarded with a kick to his chest that left him gasping.

He took a deep breath and exhaled, his gaze latching onto the two perfect crescent-moons of creamy flesh peeking out from under that skimpy skirt-and-shorts-thing she was wearing. He stifled a groan, and then silently admonished himself, averting his gaze as much as was possible and still see what he was doing. *Just get the woman out of the window!*

As he wrapped his hands around her waist, he grazed the heated skin of her stomach under the sweater. He felt rather than heard her sharp intake of breath and held his own as he secured a less intimate hold on her hips. He gave a light tug and realized the effort hadn't moved her at all.

Her skin was warm beneath the thin fabric. And she smelled good. Like musky soap and some sort of flowery shampoo. Ignoring the electricity coursing through his veins, Michael muttered aloud, "Keep your mind on the work, man." He tugged again, this time a little harder. She didn't budge.

"You really are stuck!" He couldn't help his laughter. Her heel grazed his shoulder and he was grateful he couldn't hear her angry reply.

"Okay! Okay!" he soothed. "We'll get you out. But you've got to calm down." He stepped up onto the toilet seat and held Laurel once more around the waist. Each pull on the shapely human cork caused him to chuckle harder until he was shaking with laughter.

Suddenly the toilet seat cover slipped, toppling him off-balance. He grabbed at Laurel in a vain effort to keep from falling. The forcefulness of his yank pulled Laurel from the window, her head thumping softly on the casing before they tumbled to the floor in a sprawling heap.

Aware of the hard body beneath her, Laurel scrambled to her feet. "Get out of here!" she demanded as she backed into the tiny space between the toilet and the wall.

Michael ignored the order, resting his weight on his elbows and giving himself time to catch his breath. He stared at her slim ankles a second. Then his gaze slowly traveled up her legs, noting a scrape on her knee, then continuing on to delicious-looking thighs. Lord, they were gorgeous!

She crossed her arms in an effort to hide her tight clothing, but he remembered the feel of her hips and tiny waist in his hands. Her still-damp hair fell about her shoulders in tumbled disarray. But when he looked into her emerald eyes, they were spitting fire.

Her obvious ire tripped his own defenses on. Why was she so angry? And who was she? He sat up. "Just what the hell are you doing in my house?"

"*Your* house?" She stared at him for the shortest moment, then her face paled with understanding. "You're Jim's uncle?"

"Cousin. I'm Jim's cousin." He rubbed the back of his neck, checking for soreness. "You know Jim?"

"He was supposed to call and let you know we were coming. He didn't call?"

Michael shook his head.

"I'm sorry," she said, her tone soft as a whisper.

"About...everything. Really, I am. This has turned into such a mess."

Apparently agitation had her wiping her palms down her too-short skirt.

"I feel awful about this," she continued. "I'm Laurel Morgan. Jim works for my father."

He watched her shift her weight on her feet; then she reached up and touched the back of her head. She winced.

"Are you okay?" Michael stood, not taking his eyes off her face. Once she'd nodded, he said, "I don't understand. Where's Jim?"

Laurel remembered that she must look pretty ludicrous. The sweater's tag poked into her chin, letting her know that not only had she put the top on inside out, she had put it on backward, as well. Looking down, she saw Ginny's sock flop limply in front on her foot. She reached down and snatched it off.

"Look, couldn't we talk...after I'm...dressed?" She inched toward the door at every pause. "I won't be a minute."

His only response was a curt nod as he stepped aside to let her pass, but he was sure she didn't even see it as fast as she'd scampered out of the bathroom.

Hearing the bedroom door close with a soft click, he breathed a sigh of relief. His heart beat faster just thinking of the smooth skin of her taut stomach under his fingertips. A wicked grin spread across his face as he pictured those creamy legs dangling from the window, and he knew it was a sight he'd never forget. Michael glanced up at the narrow window and shook his head. How she ever thought she could fit through that opening was beyond him.

Laurel sat huddled on the bed, a miserable wreck. How could she have made such a fool of herself? Getting stuck in a window, for heaven's sake! She rolled her eyes thinking of the picture she must have made.

Pushing the embarrassing image aside, she stripped out of Ginny's clothes and dug into her suitcase, pulling out panties and a sweatshirt. Like it or not, she had to go out and face him. Sliding the soft cotton over her head, she grimaced at the soreness on the back of her skull, in her shoulders and ribs. Would she ever be able to live this down?

She searched through the rumpled clothes, pulling out a pair of blue jeans. She hadn't had a chance to unpack and wondered if she'd even get to at all now. She'd treated Jim's cousin terribly, rewarding his offer of help with the flat tire with outright rudeness. And she'd given him a good, solid kick just a few minutes ago.

The denim raked against her scraped knee and she inhaled sharply. She jerked off the jeans and tossed them on the bed, substituting a pair of worn, fleecy sweatpants instead. She stuffed her feet into socks as her mind conjured excuses for her behavior; he had looked rough when they'd first met. And dirty. And that rifle hanging in his truck window had frightened her. Two women traveling alone couldn't be too careful these days. Add to that Ginny's recount of his review of her body and it was enough to make anyone jump to the wrong conclusion. Wasn't it?

Well, wasn't it?

Her sigh was full of self-reproach. He may have been scraggy and whiskered, but now that she thought about it, he hadn't been a bit threatening. That had been the work of her overactive paranoia.

She yanked a comb through her thick, damp hair. Knowing it would be unruly if she didn't blow it dry, she quickly sectioned it and worked the strands into a single thick braid.

She stood with her hand on the doorknob feeling extremely timid. Should she try to talk him into letting them stay or let him throw her out on her ear as she deserved? Taking a deep breath, she slowly opened the door. She saw he had helped himself to a glass of iced tea.

He looks as embarrassed as I feel, she thought. Surprised by that, she tried to smile, wanting to put him at ease.

He set his glass on a table, then said sheepishly, "I'm sorry I disturbed your shower."

Was that an understatement! She clamped her lips shut in an effort to suppress the all-out-grin struggling to take over her face. But the smile won the battle. Then a tiny chuckle forced itself out. She placed one hand over her mouth, the other on her stomach, and found herself helpless once again, this time to laughter.

"I'm sorry." Raising her eyes to his, she saw he was trying valiantly to wrestle down his own amusement.

"You really were stuck." He, too, finally gave way to laughter.

"Like a cork in a bottle," she wailed.

"I thought the same thing!"

They both bent forward slightly, their laughter filling the room.

Finally, Michael approached her, reaching out his hand. "I'm Michael Walker, Jim's cousin and the owner of this humble abode."

She found his grasp as warm and friendly as his laugh. His handsome face showed an amicable openness, and she wondered why she hadn't seen it from the start. Again she regretted her earlier treatment of him.

"I really am sorry," she felt compelled to say as she held onto his hand.

"It's okay. I looked pretty bad earlier." His lips tilted at one corner as he added, "Bad enough to give anyone the wrong impression."

They both realized in the same instant that the handshaking had long since stopped, and they simultaneously released their hold. Awkwardly, he jammed his hands into his pockets. She clasped hers behind her back.

"You were bleeding when you left the bathroom," he said. His eyes darted to her knee, then back to her face. "And you took a pretty sharp bump on the head. Are you okay? Do you want some ice?"

Those dark eyes seemed to search for her soul.

"The scrape is nothing," she murmured. "It'll be fine. And my head's pretty hard. At least, that's what my sister says, anyway."

It was difficult to believe this smartly dressed, soft-spoken man and the dirty, gruff one who had scared her so were one and the same. The thick growth of whiskers that had covered his face had hidden the strength of his jaw. But those dark, piercing eyes were exactly as she remembered them. No amount of grime could have clouded that intense gaze.

"Is something wrong?"

"Oh, no." She dipped her chin and stared at the floor, embarrassed and appalled by her unintentional inspection of him. "Uh, I was just wondering..." She focused on his face and saw him patiently waiting for her to finish. "When you stopped earlier, why did you look so..." She searched for the right word.

"Rough?" he offered. Then he shrugged. "I'd been out camping. I like to challenge myself to live off the land for a few days a couple of times a year. I always come back half-starved to death." He grinned. "You can only survive on roots and berries so long."

"Then Jim probably did call and wasn't able to reach you."

"Probably," he agreed. "I always lock my cell phone in the glove compartment so I have it in case of an emergency. But when I camp, I like to be as technology free as possible."

She nodded, and after a quiet moment, asked, "Well, do you mind? That we're here? I mean, will our staying a couple of weeks cause a problem?"

"It's just that I expected Jim home for the wedding." Halfway through his sentence she heard a muted beep. He reached into his pocket, took out his phone and flipped it open.

"I'm on call tonight," he told her, scanning the

screen. "And apparently there's a problem. Excuse me one second, I need to call the office."

Laurel watched him punch a couple of buttons. As he talked, she studied his profile. His jaw was square and contrasted nicely with the angle of his cheekbone. An ever so slight groove rested in the middle of his chin below perfectly shaped lips. She was mesmerized watching them contract and relax as he formed the words of his conversation, and she wondered if they would feel soft and warm on her own. She snapped out of her daydream as he slid the cell phone closed and tucked it into his pocket. She had to force herself not to look away when his eyes met hers.

"There's an emergency. I have to run," he said quietly.

"You're a doctor?"

"No," he said, smiling at her question. "I'm a park ranger for Garrett County. A few families are staying in the park and a smoke alarm in one of the cabins went off." He raked a hand restively through his dark brown hair and glanced toward the door. "It's probably nothing. Ten to one someone burned their fish dinner or forgot to open the chimney damper." His smile widened. "City folks do that sort of thing all the time."

Watching his purposeful strides as he walked out the door, Laurel shook her head, still amazed by how different he looked now than he had earlier on the side of the road. Shouldn't she have realized he was okay? That he posed no danger to her and Ginny?

And what was that he had said about a

wedding? She stepped out onto the porch and returned his parting wave. Sighing, she thought that it was just as well that he was taken; there wasn't room in her life for a man, anyway.

She saw Ginny coming up the lane. As the two vehicles passed, Laurel smiled at her sister's stunned expression.

"That was..." She balanced a pizza box on one hand, pointing at the departing truck with the other.

"I know, I know."

"Well, what was he doing here?" Ginny's eyes were wide with curiosity.

"Bring that pizza inside and I'll tell you the whole horrible story. I hope you got the works."

Ginny's eyes grew larger with each embarrassing detail. But Laurel didn't mind sharing them with her. They were having the most intimate conversation they'd had in months. It was like old times between them again.

"I can't believe it!" Ginny laughed, clearly delighted.

Laurel muttered, "Well, believe it."

"I can't believe you honestly thought you could fit through that window! I would have given anything to have seen it all."

"Ginny!"

They broke into a fit of giggles.

A few minutes later, Laurel nibbled on a piece of pizza crust. "This is so nice." She stretched her legs out toward the fireplace and wiggled her bare toes a comfortable distance from the heat of the crackling flames.

"It reminds me of that slumber party I had a long time ago." Ginny sighed. "Do you remember?"

"Are you kidding me?" Laurel crossed her arms behind her head. "Mom had been sick about three months and I knew it was getting you down, so I wanted to do something special for your birthday."

"You invited ten of my friends over—"

"I should have made it five," Laurel interrupted.

Ginny laid her head back on the couch and spoke dreamily, "We stayed up all night talking."

"Or three. It took me two days to clean up the popcorn."

"That was one of the nicest things you ever did for me." Ginny turned her head to look at her sister. "I never told you this, but I was scared then."

Laurel sat up, tucking her feet under her, ready to listen.

"It was like having two deaths in the family instead of one. Brian drowned, and the same day Mom left in an ambulance. I didn't see her for weeks." Ginny stared into the glowing firelight. "When she did come home she wasn't the same." The reminiscence filled Ginny's eyes with sadness. "She's never been the same."

"I know, honey." The lump in Laurel's throat made it difficult to speak.

"It's like living with a ghost the way she floats around the house, quiet and staring."

Laurel was silent, not knowing what to say. Their mother's depression had left a shadow of the woman she once was.

"Brian's death made Mom—" Laurel searched for the right word "—fragile."

Ginny's smile was soft. "That sounds like Dad talking."

"It is," Laurel confessed.

"And Dad really promised to stay with Mom?"

Laurel nodded. "Don't look so surprised. Jim is there to help. They'll do all right."

"You know," Ginny informed her, scowling, "that all those business trips Dad takes are just a cop-out, a way for him to get away from all of our family problems. Brian dying. Mom." She paused, then her voice dropped to a hoarse whisper as she added, "And me."

"Don't be ridiculous." Laurel knew her aim at nonchalance was awkward. She was surprised by Ginny's perception and didn't want her sister to be hurt by their father's ineptitude.

"But it's not fair," Ginny stated flatly. "It's not fair to any of us, you, me or Mom."

"Gin, you can't think of it as fair or unfair," Laurel tried to explain. "You shouldn't expect more from a person than they're able to give. And the rest you just have to learn to deal with."

A silence followed in which both of them were lost in their own thoughts.

The rest you deal with. Laurel knew that she had been given a lot to deal with in her life. But she had never viewed it as unfair. So what if she had to work a little harder to keep her family healthy and happy? She loved them and it was worth it.

"You know what was strangest of all?" Ginny

slowly twirled a strand of hair around her index finger. "Having my older sister go to my parent-teacher conferences. That was just plain weird."

"Well—" Laurel shrugged "—with Dad working and Mom sick, somebody had to make you toe the line."

"You did that all right!" Taking a sip of soda, Ginny continued, "You never missed one of my concerts. Or the school play."

"You were good in that," Laurel complimented her. She took a bite of pizza, then teased, "Snow White and the Seven Dwarfs, right?"

"Laurel," Ginny reprimanded. "It was the Shoemaker and the Elves! I played the shoemaker's wife."

"I knew it had little people in it." Laurel wiped her greasy fingertips on a paper napkin. "It was hilarious. All those gangly teenagers walking on their knees."

Ginny ignored the gibe. "We wanted to do something exotic like South Pacific or Hair, but Mrs. Ross said, 'Stick to a fairy tale, children,'" Ginny mimicked the old teacher with a high, cracking voice. "We did everything—wrote the script, made the set and costumes. We were even responsible for refreshments."

"It was a big job. Your class pulled it off just fine."

"We did," Ginny agreed. "Oh, we had our setbacks, but it turned out great." Grabbing another lock of hair, Ginny sighed wistfully. "High school was great."

Not missing a beat, Laurel said, "Speaking of school..."

Determined that Ginny would not be forced into the family business as she had been, Laurel desperately wanted her sister to expand her horizons, to go as far as her dreams could take her.

"Oh, no." Ginny pulled a frown. "Not again! Look, Laurel, I told you already. You're not going to push me into college."

Laurel watched her sit up and cross her arms protectively over her chest.

"Ginny, what is it you want to do with your life?"

"I don't know!"

Laurel patiently said, "You can't go on the way you have been."

"What's wrong with the way I've been?" Ginny's lips were stubbornly taut. "Wait! Let me answer that!"

Laurel didn't want to fight. They'd shared such a wonderful evening. But, looking at her sister's face, she knew it was too late, that all she could do now was suffer the storm.

"I'm wild and uncontrollable, right?" Ginny glared. "And you're worried. And Dad's worried. And Mom. *Ha!* Mom." Her bitter voice shook with emotion. "She's not even aware of her evil daughter, now, is she?"

This outpouring of hostility surprised Laurel. She stared at her sister a long moment before saying, "You're not evil. I don't think that and neither does Dad."

"What do you think?" Without giving her a

chance to respond, Ginny plowed on. "I suppose everyone wants me to be like you—Miss Mature, Miss Responsible." Anger reddened her face. Her shoulders were square and tight.

"Why do you say those words like they're dirty?"

"I knew it!" Ginny spat out.

"Calm down," Laurel softly pleaded.

"I am calm!" Taking a deep breath, Ginny stated, "Okay, let's examine your mature, responsible life-style."

"Now wait just a minute. We're talking about your life, not mine," Laurel argued.

"No, I'm serious," Ginny insisted. "I say we talk about what a wonderfully full life you lead." She paused for effect, then pointed accusingly. "You don't want to because you know what a bunch of baloney it is. Your life is so wrapped up in me and Dad and Mom and the shop that you don't have a friend in the world!"

"That's not true. Jim—"

"Jim doesn't count, Laurel! He works for Dad. That's the only reason you even know him." Ginny was thoroughly disgusted. "Face it! You have no fun. Your life is boring with a capital B. *Boring!*"

Laurel looked down at the napkin in her hands and saw that she had pulled it to shreds. She hated to admit it, but some of what her sister said was true. She managed Seashell Cove, their family-owned gift shop, because, after her brother's death and her mother's breakdown, her father needed her.

She'd wanted to go to college, to pursue a

career in education. But as her family's need of her had become greater and greater, her hopes of ever getting her teaching credentials had dwindled. Instead, she had become Ginny's surrogate mother, her mother's nursemaid and her father's confidante and business partner.

Resigned to the fact that she'd never continue her education, Laurel took care of her family the best way she knew how: loving them, looking after them, thinking of them every minute of every day. But she had never thought it a burden. On the contrary, she was more than happy to give them everything they needed, help them in any way possible.

"My life is full," she said in her defense. But why did the words sound so hollow, so unconvincing?

"Your life may be full, but it's boring! You never have a good time. I don't even think you know how. You don't have any friends. You don't go out with guys. When was the last time you had a date? Your senior prom?"

"I can have just as good a time as anyone." Laurel bristled. Ginny's last remark had hit home. She'd dated several men, summer vacationers who had wanted more of her time than she could give. She had found them immature and irresponsible. One of them had even had the gall to make a joke about her mother. After that she refused all offers to go out, not wanting to waste her time with such childishness.

Trying to change the subject, Laurel asked, "Why is it you equate having a good time with dating men?"

Ginny ignored the question and persisted. "Give me one example."

"Of what?" Laurel asked, her eyes narrowing warily.

"Of you having a good time." There was a teasing glint in the teen's eye.

Laurel sat, silent.

"I only asked for one." Ginny chuckled. "All I'm saying is I am not you. You can't expect me to live like you do." She rolled her eyes. "My social life would be pushing up daisies!"

"Your social life." Laurel jumped in with both feet. "That's what we're supposed to be discussing here."

"But what we've both discovered is that it's *your* social life that needs work."

"I've discovered no such thing." Laurel walked around the couch.

"Are you up for a bet?" Ginny's face was mischievous.

Laurel had a sinking feeling in her stomach.

"You show me that you can have a good time." Ginny twisted her body around and rested her elbows on the back of the couch. "And I'll..." She paused, thinking of the right phrase. "I'll think about college."

"What do you mean, show you I can have a good time?" Laurel asked suspiciously.

She watched as Ginny turned around, plopped down on the cushion and rubbed her chin. "Well, let's see."

Laurel closed her eyes and shook her head. She

was in big trouble. Opening her eyes, she saw Ginny's excitement.

"For the next two weeks," the younger girl gleefully explained, "throw caution to the wind! Have a good time. Meet some men, go out on a few dates." She wickedly wiggled her eyebrows up and down. "Maybe even fool around a little." She laughed at the horrified expression on her sister's face. "You'd think I said a bad word."

Laurel snapped her mouth shut and thought fast. "I don't know whether or not you've noticed," she said with a smug smile, "but we're out in the middle of the woods. Where, pray tell, are we going to find any men?"

"Guys are around," Ginny shrugged. "We'll find them, don't worry."

"I don't like how you said that. Like you're some kind of expert."

"Well."

"Never mind! I don't want to know." Laurel scowled.

"We could always round up that gorgeous cousin of Jim's." Ginny's grin was infectious.

"Ginny." Laurel couldn't help but chuckle. "You sound like you're herding cattle."

"In a way, we are," she said with an impish smirk. "We'll have him hog-tied before he knows it. He'll never know what hit him."

"Well, cowpoke, I have some news for you." Sauntering a few steps, Laurel said, "That bull's already been branded."

"Oh? He's married?"

"Not yet. But he will be soon, though. He expected Jim home for the wedding." Then she speculated, "Maybe Jim's going to be his best man." Staring into the wavering shadows the fire cast across the room, she was bewildered by the tiny tug of dismay that the thought of his wedding caused inside her. Impatiently, she shook off the feeling, bringing her thoughts back to her present problem.

Laurel studied her sister's peachy complexion and her long silky blond mane and thought that someone who didn't know Ginny would think she was an angel.

"Well, is it a deal or what?"

"Don't rush me. I need to think about this a minute." Laurel heaved a sigh. Heaven knew she'd tried everything to make her see reason short of locking Ginny in the basement. Laurel thought of all the lectures she'd doled out that had gone unheeded. Maybe it was time to change tactics.

"Now, let me get this straight." Laurel picked up the poker and jabbed at the fire, sending glowing ashes swirling up the chimney. "All I have to do is show you I can have a good time?"

"You have to fraternize with the opposite sex."

Ginny's bluntness made Laurel grimace. It wasn't that she didn't like men. Men were fine. A necessary part of the human race. It was just that she was a bit rusty where men were concerned.

Rusty? That didn't even begin to describe her.

"If I'm not able to?" Laurel asked.

"Then you'll keep your nose out of my life," Ginny retorted.

"And if I win this bet? If I have what you call 'a good time'?" Laying the poker down, she faced Ginny with her question.

"Then I'll think about my future."

"College?" Laurel challenged.

"I'll think about college." Ginny's confident look said that this was something that would never happen.

Laurel mused. How hard could it be? Go out to dinner a couple of nights, maybe a movie or two. It might even be fun.

A slow sardonic smile played on her lips as she said, "You're on."

~ ~ ~

Laurel awoke with a start, aware of only one thing, the bone-chilling cold. She pulled at the quilt and drew herself into a ball, trying to stop the violent shaking, but warmth evaded her.

Dawn was beginning to light the sky. She crept out of bed, the floor like ice on her already frozen feet. Groping for her robe and a pair of wool socks, she shivered uncontrollably. The fire in the living room hearth had died to a soft orange glow.

Removing the screen that protected the floor against sparks, she placed the last chunk of wood on top of the ashes. Adding a piece of wadded newspaper, she gently blew on the embers, bringing the fire crackling back to life.

After slipping into her sneakers, Laurel stepped onto the porch on her way to the woodpile. She paused at the eerie beauty that met her eyes. A thin lacy fog slowly danced and swirled in silent abandon around the trees and bushes of the forest. The screen door creaked as it slid from her fingers.

A sudden movement on the porch made her stop. Not three feet from her was a skunk. He, too, had stopped and was curiously sniffing in her direction.

"Ohh...I think I'm in trouble," she whispered.

Inching her way back to the front door, she spoke quietly to the animal.

"Stay as long as you like. The porch is all yours."

She slipped back inside and closed the door with a sigh of relief. She glanced at the fire and decided the chunk of wood would last a while yet. Biting her bottom lip, she grinned at her first successful encounter with nature and padded to the kitchen for a mug of hot tea.

Ginny was still snoring in the loft after Laurel had showered and dressed. Knowing a herd of elephants couldn't wake her sister, Laurel went about straightening up the tiny cabin. That didn't take long and she found herself pacing from bedroom to kitchen to sitting room. She was so used to being constantly busy that she didn't know what to do with herself.

Relax! she scolded silently. *You're on vacation.*

Moving to the bookcase, she chose a book and sat down, propping her feet up. Forty Years in the Life of a Hunter turned out to be a fascinating account of one man's life in Garrett County. Meshock Browning lived in the early 1800s, she learned, and was a famous hunter of deer and bear right here in this very area. Resting the book on her chest, she pictured Michael as a rough and rugged hunter.

She wondered what it would be like out in the wild with him: eating fresh grilled fish over a camp fire, or sharing wild berries, or snuggling deep into a soft warm sleeping bag, his hands and lips on her body.

That last errant thought made her gasp softly and set her heart racing. She lifted the book and tried to concentrate on the words, but thoughts of Michael Walker kept intruding. The vivid description she read of the beautiful Appalachian Mountains made her eager to experience them for herself, and a nice long walk was sure to vanquish her unsettling thoughts. She closed the old book and gently placed it back on the shelf.

She grabbed her jacket and left the cabin. Taking care that the skunk was nowhere around, she chose a path and started walking. The sun glistened through lacy wet spider webs and sparkled on diamonds of dew clinging to the tips of wild ferns. The calm serenity of the forest was majestic, glorious, almost holy. But the tranquility of the forest didn't extend itself to Laurel as doubts and confusion of another kind tumbled over her.

Had she done the right thing in accepting this silly bet with Ginny? She wasn't sure. She plucked a long weed growing along the path and ran her hand over its feathery tendrils.

If it took a bet to make Ginny think about college, then Laurel was happy to accept it.

A smile smoothed her lips into a delicate curve

as she thought of her sister's suggestion of Michael as a possible candidate for "fooling around." His face came to her in a crystal clear image: dark lashes fringing laughing eyes, that little cleft in the chin of his handsome face. And she was sure his strong broad shoulders would be a perfect place for a woman to lay her head. Wondering how it would feel to be enveloped by his warm embrace, she sighed heavily.

"It's too bad you're already branded, Michael Walker," she said aloud.

The rustle of underbrush caught her attention and she stopped to look around. A raccoon was scratching at the ground, and she crouched down to watch the furry bandit as it stretched and climbed atop a tree stump. The animal's black-and-white-ringed tail was so long that, as it hung over the edge of the rotting wood, it almost touched the ground.

"Beautiful," Laurel whispered.

Moving slightly to the left get a better look, she inhaled sharply as a hand clamped down on her shoulder, pushing her roughly to her knees.

Chapter Three

She stifled a scream, her heart pounding in her chest.

"Shh," a male voice whispered in her ear.

Jerking herself loose from his grasp, Laurel twisted around to see Michael's face two inches from her own. Exhaling sharply, she glared at him.

"You scared the living daylights out of me!"

"Shh!" He watched the raccoon closely. The animal was alert, staring in their direction, and he warily sniffed the air before returning to his search for breakfast. They silently watched it for several moments.

"Isn't he cute?" Laurel finally whispered. Michael seemed not to hear, so intent was he on the raccoon.

Suddenly aware of Michael's chest pressing tightly against her arm, she grew warm as the heat of him penetrated her thin jacket. Every nerve in her body came alive. Turning her head toward him once more, she lifted her chin slightly. She closed her eyes and breathed deeply, filling her lungs with the woodsy scent of him. She felt surrounded by his presence. The steady pressure of his body against hers gave her an unbelievable sense of security. She fought desperately against the strong, almost overpowering, urge to relax against him. Her eyes snapped open as he moved away from her. She turned her head away, surprised and embarrassed that she felt shaky. Laurel desperately hoped he didn't notice the trembling that his closeness caused her. A quick, anxious glance at his face assured her she was safe, that his concentration was focused strictly on the raccoon. Then she noticed the rifle he was carrying and watched in disbelief as he slowly raised it to his shoulder.

The warm security inside her chilled to an icy horror as she saw him take aim at the defenseless animal. Without thinking, she grabbed the barrel of the gun, shoving it down hard toward the ground. "No!"

The scream frightened the raccoon and it scampered into the thick underbrush.

"What the devil did you do that for?" He stood and angrily reset the safety on the rifle. "Do you realize that I've been tracking that animal for over two hours?"

Laurel jumped to her feet, her eyes fixed on him in a stern glare.

"You were going to shoot that poor thing!" she accused him, then jeeringly added, "What a big, mighty hunter you are!"

"Tranquilize!" He shook the gun. "I was going to tranquilize 'that poor thing'!"

The anger she felt drained from her body like water gurgling from a wide-mouthed bottle. Standing there dazed and numb, she watched as his irritation seemed to dissolve with a heavy sigh.

"Look, raccoons are strictly nocturnal animals." He spoke to her with the exaggerated patience one would use on a child. "That means if you see one out during the day, it's probably sick, maybe even rabid. It could very well be a threat to the other animals in the area. I was going to tranquilize that animal, cage it and have it watched."

Laurel was mortified. She'd done it again. Every single time she met this man she acted asinine. "I'm sorry." Miserable, she looked down at the ground and swallowed convulsively. It took all the courage she could muster to look him in the eye. "I didn't know."

Once again lowering her gaze, she wondered what it was about this man that left her feeling so uncertain, so inadequate. She, who single-handedly managed a successful business, who took excellent care of a sick parent and practically raised her younger sister, never felt incompetent. Not until she met Michael Walker, that is.

He curled his fingers under her chin and gently lifted until their eyes locked. "It's okay." His smile was kind, his look oddly intense and full of tender warmth.

His thumb softly caressed the silky skin of her jaw, then he bent and placed a light kiss on the corner of her mouth. "These forests and creatures mean a lot to me." His voice was quiet, almost reverent. "It's nice to know someone else cares as much as I do." He lightly smoothed her furrowed brow and added, "Don't worry, he won't hide for long."

Laurel felt her brows draw together as she watched him tramp off in the same direction the raccoon had taken. Her frown wasn't caused by worrying about the animal. In fact, she'd forgotten all about it. Her frown was due to a much different reason.

His kiss had caught her off guard, his soft, warm lips barely touching hers before it was over. Not having time to savor the moment had been frustrating, but what confused her was the warm tingling, something akin to electricity, that skittered across her breasts and downward, urging her to lean forward and slide her arms around him. But, thank goodness, she hadn't had time to act before he'd pulled away. And afterward, as he stared at her, his heavy-lidded eyes seemed filled with...

With what? If she didn't know better, she'd say desire. But that's impossible, she thought. Ridiculous, even. The man was going to be married. Shaking her head and shrugging her shoulders, she shook herself out of this silly sentimentality and passed his quirky behavior off as gratitude. She had shown concern over one of his forest creatures. That's all it was. That's all it could have been.

But as she walked back along the path toward the cabin, the frown remained, furrowing deep creases in her brow.

~ ~ ~

Glancing at her sister swaying in time to the music, Laurel turned the knob of the car radio, reducing the volume of the only rock station Ginny could find.

"Tonight I'm going to teach you the meaning of the words 'good time.'" Ginny shimmied her shoulders and laughed.

Holding back the dubious retort that threatened to spill off the tip of her tongue, Laurel placed both hands back on the steering wheel and stared out at the road as far as the headlights would allow. Driving along the narrow winding mountain road during the day had made her nervous. At night it terrified her. However, the road conditions were only one reason she was driving like a little old lady on her way to church. She'd more than once experienced reservations about tonight and wasn't sure that she should be participating in this wager at all. But she'd tried everything else. If this was the only way to get her sister to consider college, she'd play Ginny's game.

"We'll never get into town if you don't speed it up a little," Ginny complained.

"Just be patient," Laurel said, not taking her eyes off the road. "These roads are dangerous."

"I know what you're trying to do."

Picturing the impish grin on Ginny's face, Laurel slowed the car to a crawl to turn a particularly hazardous curve.

"You're trying to get out of our bet." Ginny paused only an instant before she shrugged and said, "That's fine with me. You just remember not to pester me again about college."

"I am not trying to get out of the bet." Not wanting Ginny to notice her misgivings, she smirked. "In fact, I may teach you a thing or two." Stopping at a traffic light on the edge of town, she turned to Ginny with a sly smile, then chuckled at her sister's surprised expression.

"Yes." Laurel grinned. "We may discover that I have an untapped talent for having fun. So, stand back, Oakland, here I come!"

They drove along the dark and empty main street through the small, seemingly desolate town.

"Not much going on, is there?" Laurel finally asked.

"Nothing, I'd say." Disappointment rounded Ginny's shoulders to a slump.

"Oh, come on now. Don't give up so easily." Laurel turned the car down a side street and pointed. "Look there. Lights, people. This could be promising."

The tires crunched on the gravel lot as Laurel found a parking space at the end of a row. Removing the keys from the ignition, she studied her sister's discouraged expression in the shadows.

"What's the problem?"

Ginny scowled at the door of the building. "1 can't believe that all this town has to offer on a Saturday night is bingo at the local fire hall."

"Would you come on!" Laurel unhooked her seat belt then reached over to give her sister's shoulder a nudge. "You don't know that it's bingo. And, who knows, bingo might be fun." She opened her door and mumbled under her breath, "It's certainly more my speed than what *you* had on the agenda for tonight."

As the women stepped out of the car a faint tune drifted out to them, perking Ginny up immediately. "This may not be so bad after all," she said.

A large sign posted at the door read Welcome! Autumn Glory Festival Kickoff Dance.

The large, brightly lit room was filled with people of every age. Rows of trestle tables were filled with an array of mugs, glasses, soda cans, beer pitchers and plastic cups. The band was doing its best to ruin a well-known pop tune, but the crowd didn't seem to mind. Loud laughter and an open spirit of camaraderie permeated the air.

"How about if I get us a beer?" Ginny's eyes sparkled with excitement.

"I'll have soda, thanks. And so will you."

"Party pooper!"

Laurel took an empty seat and watched her sister cruise up to the bar. Almost immediately, Ginny was approached by a tall, blond teenager. Her laughing features tilted up to his as they talked. Laurel sighed and turned to face the band.

I'm going to be a terrible failure at this, she thought. Ginny was completely comfortable laughing with strangers, striking up conversations that led to evenings filled with casual fun. Could she do that? Nope. Strangers made her nervous and loud music gave her a headache. Yes, indeed, too many years spent taking care of too many responsibilities had pretty much suffocated her fun gene.

She smiled at the thought and placed her elbow on the table, resting her head in her hand. With eyes closed, she listened as the band played a half beat behind the singer's soprano voice.

What she needed was a nice, quiet man. A man who liked to spend his evenings playing Rummy or working crossword puzzles. But how would she ever find a guy like that in a place like this? It would certainly save a lot of trouble if he would find her....

Laurel smile widened as Michael's rugged image immediately appeared in her mind. Not wanting to admit that she'd made a fool of herself again, she hadn't told Ginny about meeting him on the path that morning. Her heart beat faster as she recalled his taut muscles and the heat she'd felt when his body touched hers. Remembering his kindhearted disregard of her rashness concerning the raccoon, she felt a warmth curl in her stomach even now. If only his lips had stayed on hers a while longer. If only she could have had time to respond!

She chuckled, then silently chided herself. *He's already taken.* Sighing, she twisted around to see what was taking her sister so long.

Ginny was still talking with the tall blond, and Laurel sat up straighter when she saw that Michael had joined them. She watched as her sister pointed in her direction and Michael's gaze followed.

"Oh, God," Laurel moaned as he strolled over. "I am not going to look like an idiot this time."

Smiling easily, he set a soda down by her arm and took the seat next to her.

"Hello."

She nodded a greeting, afraid that if she opened her mouth she might have to pry her foot out of it.

"I saw your sister up at the bar and told her I'd bring you your soda. I hope you don't mind."

Laurel only smiled in answer.

"I wanted you to know that I caught the raccoon. I heard from the vet this evening. It was sick and had to be put down."

"Oh." The word came from the back of her throat, low and sad.

"Don't worry. It didn't feel any pain." Michael placed his elbow on the table and swirled his frothy beer in his mug.

Laurel watched, transfixed, as he took a deep swallow, and she had to curl her fingers into a fist to fight the urge to reach out and touch muscle and sinew of his tanned throat.

"With the shape that raccoon was in," he continued, "it could have made a lot of other animals sick."

It was then that Ginny pulled out a metal chair, its legs grating loudly against the tile floor, and plopped down across from Laurel. Three other teenagers joined her at the table and she introduced Laurel to them all.

The name of the tall blond mooning over Ginny was Eric. Laurel was mildly surprised to hear from the conversation that he was eighteen. Despite his height, his slim shoulders and lanky build looked more suited to a boy much younger. Sitting next to Michael's manly brawn, she mused, put Eric at a distinct disadvantage. The girls' names were Sharon and Nancy.

When a lively song began to play, Eric asked

Ginny to dance, and after they left the table Laurel and Michael talked to the two girls who stayed behind.

"So, Sharon, what are your plans now that you've graduated?" Michael directed his query to the plump brunette sitting across from him.

"I'm going to do some traveling," she said, barely able to contain her boisterous energy. "My grandmother lives in California. I'll be going to visit her right after Thanksgiving. As soon as I save enough money, though, I'm going to go *every*where, see *every*thing."

"How about you, Nancy?" Laurel asked the other girl.

"I'm a freshman at Frostburg State." Nancy's demeanor was shy, her voice soft. "I'm majoring in elementary education. I love kids, and I've always wanted to teach. I can't think of anything more important than educating this country's children." Realizing her impassioned tone, she blushed crimson.

"She comes home to visit me every weekend, since the university's only an hour away." Sharon glanced at her friend, her brow furrowing. "I don't know what we'll do when I go away."

Laurel smiled, thinking the two girls couldn't be more different. Sharon's rambunctiousness was as different to Nancy's philosophic primness as night was to day. Hearing the girls talk of their hopes and dreams made Laurel feel much older than her twenty-four years. Did she ever have dreams of changing the world? Maybe once, she thought wistfully, a long time ago. Before she became so involved helping her family survive.

Eric and Ginny returned to the table completely out of breath after their vigorous dance. Sitting down, they both took long draws on their sodas. When one of the band members announced the next tune, Ginny gave Eric an almost inconspicuous nudge. The gangly teen moved closer to Laurel.

"Would you like to dance?"

"Um...uh," Laurel felt her neck and face flush hot.

The beginning beats of a slow tune drifted through the room and the lights went dim. It had been so long since she'd danced. And a slow one at that! She was sure to step on the kid's toes and end up looking like a fool. Yet, Ginny's steady gaze glistened with a taunt; it was clear the teen was sure she was going to win their bet.

"Sorry," Michael said, his warm hand closing possessively over Laurel's wrist as he spoke to Eric. "She's promised this one to me." He gently pulled her from the chair, then his hold slid from her wrist to her hand. Her skin tingled as his warm grasp surrounded her icy fingers. Propelling her to the dance floor with a firm hand on her lower back, Michael cleared a path through the throng of people.

Oh, Lord, Laurel thought. She'd have much rather looked like a fool with Eric. Glancing around, she saw the other couples on the floor begin to sway to the music.

Michael stopped and gently twirled Laurel around to face him. When she didn't move into position, he looked questioningly into her eyes.

"You look like you've been led to the gallows."

"I was just thinking that you may be sorry about this." Her mouth closed in a grim smile.

"Oh?"

"I haven't...it's been a...this isn't something..." When words finally failed her, she tried to finish the explanation with a dismal shake of her head. Slowly raising her lashes, she looked at him ruefully.

"Hey, this is supposed to be an enjoyable experience," he said, offering her an engaging smile. "Trust me."

He placed one of her hands lightly on his shoulder; the other he held in the crook of his hand. Reaching around her, he rested his other hand on the small of her back.

"Relax. I'll guide you."

Before she had a chance to react, he pulled her closer to him.

After a few tentative steps, his steady guiding pressure gave her a small semblance of confidence, and she felt the tension in her shoulders loosen. She didn't want to think about anything: making a fool of herself, or her rebel of a sister, or the problems that might be taking place back home, or anything. She only wanted to move with this man, to get lost in the crooning singer's words that complained of a life without love.

Laurel looked up into Michael's face and found his dark eyes staring at her. Unnerved by his intense gaze, she glanced over his shoulder. He pulled her closer, and it seemed the most natural thing in the world for her to rest her cheek on his shoulder.

She inhaled slowly, deeply. He smelled so good.

She watched his pulse beating in his throat and found herself wanting desperately to get closer, to press her nose directly to his skin. Noticing a short lock of his hair that curled toward his ear, she ran a finger over it lightly. It stayed in place only a moment before softly springing back. Michael let go of her hand and tugged her into an even more intimate position. Her eyes widened in surprise, but she wrapped both arms around his muscular back and hoped the song would never end. After a few slow beats, she pulled back a little and lifted her head, and she saw the same dreamy expression on his face that she was certain was on her own. She couldn't stop the smile that spread across her mouth.

"You're not as rusty as you thought," he whispered.

"Mmm," she agreed, her smile widening.

She switched positions, sliding her arms up and clasping her hands behind his neck. His gaze took on a velvety warmth even in this dim light, and she knew he was going to kiss her.

Slowly he lowered his head and covered her lips with his. The firm but gentle pressure was deliciously warm and moist. A familiar ache filled her breasts. Shuddering, she pressed against him as the ache traveled down, deep into her soul, expanding into a blazing flame that surged through her body.

A low, breathless moan escaped from the back of her throat as Michael ended the kiss. Her eyelids were heavy, and she opened them slowly, as if waking from a dreamy sleep. She sighed and looked into his passion-filled eyes.

Dimly, she became aware of the couples moving from the dance floor. The music had stopped and the lights overhead glared. She dropped her arms and stepped away from him, wondering how long they'd been standing there.

"Sorry...I don't—I—"

"Laurel." Michael cocked his head and looked at her quizzically.

Her knees were shaking and she hoped she could get back to the table without making more of a spectacle of herself. She felt him take hold of her elbow and was grateful for the support. All the way back to the table her mind was bombarded with conflicting feelings.

How could a simple dance turn into something so much more? She had become so aroused by his kiss. Had he felt the same excitement as she? Laurel had been so caught up in her own emotions she hadn't even noticed his reaction. What did he think of her for allowing such intimacy when they barely knew each other? But hadn't it been wonderful?

Michael left her at the table and went to the bar to refill their drinks. Laurel looked across to Ginny's wickedly grinning face and knew her sister hadn't missed the scene on the dance floor. Laurel grinned back stupidly. Nothing Ginny could say to her could lessen her pleasure.

"I thought you said he was already branded," Ginny said with wry amusement.

Laurel's hazy bliss slowly dissolved. Blinking twice, she stared at Ginny. What had she done? How could she have let that happen? She had completely forgotten that he was engaged. Her teeth clenched tightly. How could he do such a thing?

Nervous anger shot through her, making her feel hot and faint. Her sister reached over and, in a comforting gesture, patted her hand.

"Hey, what's a little premarital fling?" She sat back, laughing, and added with a shrug, "Who's it going to hurt? Enjoy yourself!"

"Yes, enjoy yourself!" Michael, who had returned in time to hear Ginny's last statement, set down a cold soda in front of Laurel.

She couldn't bring herself to even touch it, let alone drink it. Disappointment and guilt tangled in her gut. She glanced around the room, wondering if Michael's fiancée was there.

No, she didn't think so. Otherwise, he wouldn't have kissed her. No one could be that cold and insensitive.

"Laurel," Ginny said, leaning over the table, "the four of us want to go for pizza. Could I take the car?"

"But, um, how would I—no!" She frantically shook her head. She absolutely, positively, did not want to be left alone with Michael.

"I won't be late."

Ginny stared directly at her with a plaintive please-don't-embarrass-me look. Laurel sighed and put one hand up to her temple.

"Ginny, I'm tired," she lied. "I have a headache and I want to go home."

"Let them go." Michael's quiet voice made her

turn in his direction. He placed his hand on hers. "I'll take you home."

Her steady gaze rested on his face. Who was he to tell her what to do? This wasn't *his* sister telling them she wanted to go off gallivanting with strangers in the middle of the night. And hadn't he shown her exactly how irresponsible he was by kissing her when he was engaged to someone else?

"Please?"

Her sister's tone held a plaintive appeal. Michael offered her a what's-the-big-deal shrug. And the other teens hovered with eager expressions. Laurel felt ganged-up on, that much was sure.

Withdrawing her hand from Michael's grasp, she reached into her purse for the keys. She was *not* happy. She'd let Ginny go, and she would let Michael take her home. But he'd regret ever offering, because she planned to tell him exactly what she thought of him. Him and his 'premarital' flirting!

"Sure, go have a good time." Sliding the keys across the table to Ginny, Laurel hoped the statement didn't sound as forced as it felt. "Ginny." All four of the teens turned to hear her say, "Please don't be too late."

"I won't, I promise!" Ginny called over her shoulder as she and her newfound friends headed toward the door.

Laurel clutched her purse tightly in both fists. The tight smile she had given to Ginny vanished, replaced by a grim line. She turned severe eyes on Michael.

"I'm ready to go." Pushing her chair out, she stood up.

He also stood, placing a hand on the back of her chair.

"Sure," he said, stacking the empty cups and cans they had used. "Let me get rid of these. And I need to find Darlene. Let her know I'm leaving and see if she has a ride home."

"The bride-to-be? She's here?" she asked through a strained, unnatural smile. Her nails dug deeper into the soft leather of her handbag.

"Yeah. She's a great girl." The laugh lines on his face deepened with his smile.

Laurel cringed inside when she saw his eyes soften as he spoke of the woman.

"I'm sure she's in the kitchen. Her father's a volunteer fireman, so she helps out the ladies' auxiliary when they're shorthanded. You want to come meet her?"

"Michael—"

"I'm sure she'd love to meet you."

The whole situation was more than a little odd. He didn't seem the least bit guilty, the least bit ashamed of his behavior. Maybe they had some strange backwoods customs here regarding marriage. Whatever was going on, it was making Laurel nervous.

"Look, I'm really not in the mood to meet anyone." *Least of all your girlfriend*, she silently added. "I'm really tired. My head hurts. I want to go home. I'll meet you outside." She turned and strode toward the exit.

Michael stood, bewildered, watching her walk away from him. What was wrong with her? Jim and Darlene were going to be married soon, and they'd be moving to Ocean City. Jim had been working for Laurel's father for quite a while. Michael would have thought she'd at least want to meet Jim's fiancée. Instead she'd used some lame excuse about a headache to beg off. She'd certainly felt fine ten minutes ago while they were dancing.

He'd never met a woman more willing to be kissed. He could still feel the pressure of her quivering body as she arched against him and the warmth of her silky lips lingering on his. She hadn't noticed when the music had stopped or the lights had been turned up. He could have gone on kissing her all night, he thought, grinning.

He'd reluctantly ended the kiss, not wanting to put on a show for the town's busybodies who were most assuredly on alert for the next bit of juicy gossip. Information traveled fast in a town the size of Oakland, and he didn't want his private life to be the topic of discussion. Michael was certain Laurel wouldn't appreciate it, either. She might even end up with hurt feelings. Lord knew how those gossip-mongers had dragged Darlene through the verbal dirt in the past eight months. Sure, she and Jim had made a mistake, but they were working hard to put it right.

With Darlene once again on his mind, Michael turned toward the kitchen.

Laurel made her way across the room, her ire building with each step. How could he? What kind of sick-minded clod was he, offering to introduce her to his fiancée? The thought literally made her stomach turn.

Then again, maybe she should have let him go ahead and make the introduction, she thought wickedly. Maybe she should have met the poor woman, talked to her, told her exactly what kind of man she was marrying.

Her anger turned to flames of burning fury, and Laurel found herself wondering what type of woman would marry a man like Michael. Darlene either loved him to distraction, or was terribly desperate for some reason, or had not a shred of self-esteem.

Curiosity made her pause, and then turn around. She scanned the back of the room, hoping to get a glimpse of Michael's girlfriend. An image flashed through Laurel's mind of a mousy girl with a severe overbite and thick glasses, her hair in a severe bun. Pushing away the notion, Laurel silently admitted the girl could just as likely be a tall, statuesque blonde. But then why would she put up with...

"Oh my God!" The words tumbled out of her mouth before she could stop them.

"Beg pardon?" An elderly gentleman on his way in the door stopped beside her. "You okay, sweetie?" he asked. When she didn't answer, he touched her sleeve.

"What?" She glanced up at the old man, startled.

"You okay?" he repeated.

"Yes. I'm sorry. Yes, I'm fine. Fine," she stammered. "Thank you."

She rushed out the door, her heart beat frantically, and she gulped the cold night air into her burning lungs. Slinging the strap of her purse over her arm, she covered her mouth with the fingers of both hands and leaned her weight against the rough brick wall of the building.

Laurel closed her eyes and tried to breathe slowly and deeply, but she couldn't erase the picture of Michael and Darlene. Darlene wasn't mousy at all. She was blond. She was a beautiful blonde. A young, beautiful blonde. A *pregnant* beautiful blonde.

She swore softly. The poor girl looked twelve months pregnant! Why hadn't Michael married her already? What was he waiting for?

Opening her eyes wide, she pressed her hands to her temples. And before the events of this evening she'd decided he was so wonderful! Just then, Michael burst through the doorway and jogged several steps past her. He stopped and looked the parking lot over. Laurel walked up behind him.

"You—" she whispered.

He turned around, startled.

"—callous, cold, heartless beast."

"What?"

"You twisted, demented, coldhearted monster." Her voice rose in volume with each word. "You— you —jerk!" She poked him in the chest with the last word, then lost control. Her words tumbled out in a jumble of meaningless babble.

"You kissed me! She's pregnant! *Real* pregnant! How *could* you? Playing around. And her right there. Maybe watching! You—you. You *kissed* me!"

She was surprised and infuriated to feel tears sliding down her cheeks. She swiped them away and realized he was looking over her shoulder.

The crud! He wasn't even paying attention!

Michael casually smiled at several people who had come to the open doorway, lifting a hand to wave and nodding to let them know he had everything under control. Then he smoothly took Laurel by the elbow and propelled her toward his truck.

"I don't know what your problem is," he hissed. "But I'll thank you to remember that I live and work in this town. You, on the other hand, get to go home in two weeks."

What was wrong with her? Michael wondered. She had acted a little awkward after they had danced, but he'd thought she'd been embarrassed by the kiss they had shared. Taking her home and maybe sharing another kiss had been a pleasant thought, but now she was blubbering about kissing and playing around and pregnancy. He'd only kissed her, for God's sake!

Laurel got into the truck and let him close the door. She fumbled in her handbag for a tissue and loudly blew her nose. He got into the driver's side and turned to face her.

"Now that you've calmed down, you want to tell me what this is all about?" he asked.

"You kissed me," she said.

"You kissed me, too," he countered.

"But she's pregnant!"

He raised his eyebrows. "You're talking about Darlene?"

She nodded her head.

Michael rested his elbow on the steering wheel and opened his hand, palm up. "What does one have to do with the other?"

"You were playing around. Flirting with me!" Her words were stronger, her anger returning.

"You're doing it again!" he railed. "Talking of kissing and playing around and pregnancy! You can't get pregnant from a kiss!"

"I know that!" She glared at him indignantly.

"Then, what the hell's the problem?" he asked, frustrated by the senseless conversation.

"You are such a jerk! I don't even want you to take me home. I'd rather walk!" She opened the door, but he reached over and took hold of her wrist.

"Shut the door."

The dimly lit parking lot threw shadows across her glaring expression. She turned to him, eyes narrowed in anger.

"Shut the door, Laurel."

She obeyed his low, ominous demand.

"Thank you," he told her.

They sat in silence for a moment while Michael took a deep, calming breath.

"For the life of me I can't understand why you're so angry that I kissed you when I know that you enjoyed it as much as I did," he began. "But, if an apology will make you feel better, then I'm sorry if I was too forward. I shouldn't have kissed you."

"I'm not angry about that!" She spat the words out. "Well, I am, but—"

"Then what is the problem?" His voice rose an octave. Self-control, he reminded himself, self-control.

"Your pregnant girlfriend," she curtly replied.

"My what?" he exclaimed.

"Darlene!" she enunciated, loud and precise.

The light dawned, hitting him like a ton of bricks. She thought Darlene was his girlfriend, his pregnant bride-to-be! No wonder she was upset about his kissing her.

"Laurel, Darlene is not my girlfriend."

"Yeah, right! And I'm Little Red Riding Hood!"

"Well, let me tell you something, Red. Your problem is that you jump to conclusions too quickly. The first time we met, you'd have knocked me silly if I'd looked at you cross-eyed. And when I came to the cabin looking for my cousin, you took me for some kind of perverted rapist! And this morning you thought I was out shooting raccoons just for the sport of it."

He dragged a hand through his hair. "Now, listen to me! Jim and Darlene have lived together for a while now. They'd planned to get married as soon as Jim could find a good job. But then Darlene got pregnant. Jim still hadn't been able to land a job, so he went to the shore looking for work." He watched the outline of her pale, unblinking face.

"He called Darlene, really excited about his job with your father. He told her he'd fixed up an apartment and everything and was coming home this weekend or next to get married and then they'd go back to Ocean City to live. I don't know why Jim didn't tell you about Darlene. Or the wedding. Or the baby."

He glanced out the window. His next words were reflective, said almost to himself. "Maybe he was afraid of losing the first really good job he'd found."

Michael turned back to face her. "Look, I'm sorry you had to find out about this from me. Jim should have told you himself. But I hope it doesn't change your feelings for him. He really likes his job. And he has nothing but good things to say about your family. He needs that job! Those two kids love each other. And they'll take good care of that baby."

Silence settled over them for the longest time. She stared straight ahead, and Michael saw her swallow.

"Laurel." He spoke to her gently, but she didn't answer. "Hey," he said, and touched her shoulder. "Do you hear me? Do you believe me?"

Slowly she turned to look him. "Yes," she whispered, and immediately turned back to look straight ahead. "Would you please take me home now?" The words were murmured so quietly Michael barely heard them.

Donna Fasano

Chapter Four

Troubled thoughts tumbled through Laurel's mind. She'd done it again. Had she lost her mind? She'd jumped all over him without knowing what was going on. What an idiot. She wasn't the kind of person who jumped to conclusions. She was level-headed. She was responsible. Laurel sighed. Knowing it was all a mistake didn't make her feel any better.

The dashboard lights threw an eerie glow over the cab of the moving truck. Michael's pensive eyes never left the winding road. Glancing at him, she wondered if his thoughts were as jumbled as her own.

She scowled and silently reproved herself. Why not apologize to the man and get it over with! But what if he was too angry to forgive her? Her eyes narrowed. It was too late to worry about that now.

Looking out at the black forest, she wondered, yet again, what it was about this man that made her lose her good judgment.

"Michael?"

"Hmm?"

Without looking at him, she knew his eyes were on her. "I'm really sorry."

Silence. Seconds ticked by. She worried her

bottom lip between her teeth, her heel twitching up and down in a nervous dance as she tried to gauge just how angry he was. Jumping to the wrong conclusion was one thing, but to put on a show by screaming at him in front of those people was definitely another. He had every right to be furious.

The truck bumped along the lane that led to Jim's cabin. Michael pulled to a stop and turned off the ignition. Laurel couldn't stand the silence any longer.

"Look, I won't be here long. And while I'm here, I'll try to stay out of your way." She opened the door and started to get out, but his hand on her arm made her stop.

"Hold on. It's all right."

She turned to him as he spoke. The dim porch light threw dusky shadows across his features, making it difficult for her to read his expression.

"You're not angry?"

"No." He shook his head. "I'm not angry."

"But I yelled at you," she said. Looking down at her lap, she added, "Again."

"It wasn't really your fault. You had no way of knowing." His hand tightened on her arm, urging her to stay.

She closed the door and slid back into the seat, and then twisted her body toward him. Taking his warm hand in hers, she whispered, "You're such a nice man, Michael."

He smiled and shook his head

"No," she went on, "I mean it. You were right when you said earlier that I jump to conclusions. The first time I met you I had it in my mind to bang you on the shin with that tire iron—"

"And I was sure you'd aim for my head."

The grin in his voice gave her pause, but she continued, "And then, when you came into the house, I did think the absolute worst of you."

His chuckle provoked a clear picture in her mind of her tight situation and she couldn't help but smile. "And I'm not even going to mention that poor little raccoon." She solemnly shook her head. "But in every instance of my stupidity you've made allowances for my behavior and forgiven me."

He gave an exaggerated sigh. "I guess I am a pretty nice guy at that."

A tingle skittered up her arm when he gently squeezed her hand. His grasp was friendly and warm and it felt good.

"Michael," she said quietly, "I meant what I said. I'll try not to bother you again while we're here."

"Oh, come on now. That's nonsense. I could show you around. I live here, you know."

Laurel smiled and wondered why the thought of spending time with him pleased her so much. Stepping out of the truck, they walked to the cabin together.

"In fact," he said, "we can start tomorrow. Would you like to go on a picnic? I know a beautiful place."

"I'd love that! Thank you." The screen door creaked when he pulled it open and Laurel bent to unlock the door. "Oh," she said, straightening. "I forgot about Ginny."

"She's welcome to come along with us."

"That'd be great! I'll pack a lunch." Seeing him about to argue with her, she added, "I insist!" He grinned and acquiesced with a nod. She pushed the door open and stepped inside.

"Until tomorrow, then," he said. "I'll pick you up around noon."

She watched him turn and start toward his truck. Closing the door, she leaned against it and sighed.

"He is a nice man," she whispered.

~ ~ ~

"But he invited us both! You've got to come."

"Laurel, he only invited me to be polite," Ginny insisted. "Anyway, I have a lunch date."

"Oh?"

"With Eric." The younger girl grinned. "Don't worry, Sharon and Nancy will be with us. We're meeting some other kids and then going to the football game at the high school." Ginny walked over to the picnic basket Laurel had found in a closet and peered at the sandwiches and fruit inside. "You wouldn't want me around, anyway. What if he decided he wanted to make out?" She pulled a grape off the bunch Laurel had packed and popped it into her mouth. "I'd only be in the way."

"Cut it out. I'm too old to make out."

"You're never too old to make out." Ginny giggled. "He kissed you last night, didn't he?"

"That was nothing." Laurel hoped she placed the right amount of flippancy on the words. However, if she were forced to admit the truth, she'd have to confess that she'd tossed and turned well into the night wondering about that kiss. Why had Michael kissed her out on the dance floor? It was the answer to that question that had kept her awake. He'd kissed her because she'd practically thrown herself at him, cuddling up to him out on that dance floor, and now she was more than a little embarrassed about her behavior.

Hearing the roar of an approaching engine, Ginny went to the front window. "It's Eric! Gotta run!"

"But that sounds like a motorcycle!" Laurel had followed her into the room, wiping her hands on a towel. Ginny stopped at the door and swung around to face her sister.

"Give me a break!" Ginny rolled her eyes heavenward. "Don't worry! I'll wear a helmet. It's perfectly safe." She ran over and kissed Laurel on the cheek. "And I'll be back for dinner, honest. Have a good time with Michael."

Laurel watched through the window as Ginny strapped on a shiny red helmet that matched the one Eric wore. After Ginny hitched her leg up over the back of the bike, they tore off down the lane, throwing dirt and gravel behind them.

A worried frown creased Laurel's brow. When she had awakened to see the sun streaming through her window and hear birds chirping in the trees, she had been sure, a good night's sleep or not, that it would be a terrific day for a picnic. But now she knew she'd be fretting all day over Ginny on that motorbike.

When Laurel heard Michael's pickup outside

she was closing the wicker basket's lid. His knock sounded on the door a moment later.

"Come in!" she called.

"I hope I'm not late."

She was surprised to see him dressed in his uniform: light green shirt, olive twill trousers and shiny black boots. "Believe it or not, I was hunting all morning."

"Another raccoon?"

He laughed at her distressed expression. "No, no. Little boys this time. There are two young boys that live at the edge of the park. Their parents can't keep them out of the woods. Buck Brady even fenced his yard trying to keep his boys corralled. Buck and I hunted for them for over two hours before we found them buried in leaves. They said they ran out of ammo and were hiding from the enemy." He chuckled. "Those camouflage clothes the boys were wearing just about did us in." He shrugged, throwing his hands up. "But what can you do when a boy's hero is Rambo?"

The lines around Michael's eyes crinkled and his face lit with a dazzling smile that caused Laurel's heart to race. She forced herself to breathe slowly to control its pulsing flutter.

"I can't blame the boys, though," he admitted. "I was the same way." He glanced up toward the loft and then back at her before asking, "Is Ginny coming?"

As she explained to him about her sister's date, she couldn't keep the uneasiness out of her voice when she spoke of their mode of transportation.

"Don't worry. Eric's a responsible kid. I

wouldn't have suggested Ginny go with him last night if I didn't think he was trustworthy."

His understanding look melted her apprehension, and her chest filled with a tender warmth. She watched him pick up the basket by its handles.

"You ready?" he asked.

"One second." Laurel darted into the bedroom, where she had laid out a sweater and a small blanket. Standing by the bed, she inhaled deeply, willing herself to relax. More excitement churned in her stomach than she'd felt in a long time. A very long time.

You better be careful, girl, she thought. *He's almost too good to be true.*

The fingers brushing through her hair stopped in midair as she caught a glimpse of herself in the mirror. Frowning, she leaned closer and whispered, "Don't let things go too far."

Her eyes widened and she straightened as she realized what she'd said. Well, why not? Why shouldn't she enjoy herself for once? Forget about family responsibilities and just have a good time? She moistened her lips and grinned before turning toward the bedroom door.

"Lead the way!" she chimed, and followed Michael out into the bright sunshine.

"We can take the path out back," he told her. "The meadow I want to show you is at the top of this mountain."

"Top of the mountain?"

He chuckled. "It's not that far. Come on!"

Laurel breathed in the crisp mountain air, marveling at the kaleidoscope of color in the trees. Stretched out before her was a wild display of foliage, hues ranging from calm patches of soft violet and indigo to bright bursts of lime green, orange and red.

"Autumn is my favorite season. No matter how often I come out here, I find everything's changed," Michael said. Reaching out, he took her hand and helped her up a particularly steep incline.

"It may sound silly—" she was so reluctant to take her eyes off the vibrant autumnal scene, she wasn't paying close attention to where she was walking "—but I can almost *feel* the beauty radiating off of everything."

Although she realized they had stopped, she wasn't the least bothered. In fact, she took full advantage of the moment to feast on the lush and vivid landscape. Finally, she felt the gentle pressure of his fingers under her chin, guiding her gaze to his.

"It doesn't sound silly," he said quietly. "Beauty is radiating off of everything."

It was as though there was a complete and utter cessation of the world around her. The breeze stopped blowing, the birds went silent, the rustling tree branches seemed to go still—so lost was she in his dark, searching gaze.

For a long moment they were motionless, facing each other, the only two people in the universe.

Reluctantly, Michael tore his gaze away, tugged at her hand, and they resumed their trek along the mountain path.

He didn't know what it was about this hot-tempered redhead, but he hadn't been able to get her out of his mind. Even in his sleep he'd been haunted by erotic images of her—of the two of them. Together.

The kiss they had shared last night had blown his mind. Just thinking about it now made the blood run hot through his veins, made him want to stop right there and kiss her again. His breathing became labored, and he knew it wasn't just the hike up the mountain that was causing it.

She was everything a man could want in a woman. Full of fire and ice, she had demonstrated both to him last night; fire in her passionate kiss and ice in her frosty anger. A life spent with her would never be dull. Dropping her hand, he stopped to wipe his damp brow.

"You want to stop and rest?" He could tell she wasn't tired, but he needed a diversion, something to change the direction of his thoughts.

"No, I'm fine."

"It's not much farther. If you turn down that way—" he pointed off to the right "—in a few hundred yards you'll be at my place."

He pulled her up the last rocky rise, and when she smiled, the sun glinted in her green eyes. They walked another hundred feet and the trees opened up to a large meadow. A lone oak stood in the middle of the expanse of wispy grasses and weeds. The tree's huge gnarled branches dripped with thousands of yellow leaves tinted golden by the sun. They fluttered in endless movement in the light breeze.

"It's beautiful!" Laurel exclaimed.

"I spent a lot of time up in that tree as a boy."

"Looks like a kid-friendly oak."

While Michael spread the blanket and unloaded the wicker basket, she walked over to the edge of the field where she could see the valley below. Hundreds of swirling colors danced before her. A winding river peeked intermittently from between the foliage of the trees and bushes, the rippling water a deep blue ribbon woven through colorful fabric.

She was aware of Michael's presence behind her before she felt his hand on her shoulder. Turning her head toward him, she smiled, knowing in her heart she was glad Ginny had made other plans for the day.

"It's so peaceful."

"I think so, too," he said. "I come up here whenever I need a little peace and quiet." Looking out over the valley, he added, "I never get bored with this place. Never."

His gaze returned to her face, his eyes soft, and for a brief instant Laurel was sure he was going to kiss her. But instead, he took her hand and pulled her toward the blanket under the oak.

"Let's have lunch," he said. He watched her sit cross-legged before he settled himself against the tree trunk. Handing her a glass of white wine, his fingers brushed against her chilled hand.

"Here, this will warm you up a little."

"Thanks. Where'd this come from? I didn't pack wine." Her eyebrows knit together as she looked at the clear liquid. Alcohol was something she stayed away from. It always went straight to her head. The only time she had ever argued with her father had been after she'd had a couple of after-dinner drinks.

"No, I did." He grinned. "I slipped it in the basket when you went to get your sweater."

Bringing wine for their picnic was sweet of him, and romantic too. And she *was* chilly. One glass wouldn't kill her. She sipped, the wine warming a path down her throat as she swallowed.

Over chicken sandwiches and potato salad, she told him a little about herself and her family. Noticing how easy it was to talk to him, she told him how her mother had cut herself off from life, something Laurel rarely spoke about to anyone.

"So, that's it," he said.

"That's what?"

"That's why you treat your sister more like she's your daughter. It's a perfectly natural feeling," he remarked. "Especially if you helped raise her."

"We have a strange relationship. Since Mom's too sick to act as a parent, I've always tried to guide Ginny. But, believe me, if I get too domineering, she's quick to point out that I'm not the boss of her. Especially now."

"What do you mean, 'especially now'?"

She paused a moment. "I'm not really sure. But there are times when Ginny seems angry with all of us. Mom, Dad and particularly me. I've racked my brain trying to figure it out. She's been going out of her way to do things to upset us—running around with a bad crowd, staying out late, drinking. She plays her stereo in the middle of the night so loud that my mattress springs vibrate to the beat of the music."

Wiping her hands on a napkin, she continued, "It's the drinking that worries me most." Her voice had dropped to a whisper, and a frown creased her forehead as she looked at Michael with troubled eyes. "I don't think my mother could stand it if anything happened to Ginny."

"What does your father have to say about all of this?" Michael asked.

"Dad's not home much. He does a lot of traveling, buying merchandise for the shop. That's why Jim's been such a godsend to us. I really needed the help." She brushed her hair back with a swish of her hand. "It was Dad's suggestion that I take Ginny on vacation, to try to find out what's bothering her."

"It sounds like a good idea to me," he said. "Getting your sister away from her friends would give you a much better chance of talking to her."

Hearing his frank opinion, Laurel knew he understood. And for some reason she was filled with a warm happiness knowing he agreed with what she was doing.

"I've tried talking to her," she said dryly. "But now she's got things all twisted around."

"How so?"

"Well, when I brought up the subject of her future, Ginny immediately blew a fuse, accusing me of trying to force her into being just like me." Laurel tipped her wineglass back, sipping the last drop. "Apparently I'm as boring as American cheese."

Michael laughed heartily. "Listen to me," he said, his gaze steady. "I've known you less than forty-eight hours, and believe me, you're anything but boring!"

Feeling color rush to her face, Laurel hoped her grin hid her embarrassment. "Yes, but you met me under extenuating circumstances."

The wine, combined with Michael's intense stare, made her overly warm.

"Anyway, my sister ended up forcing me to accept a nice little wager. My end of the deal didn't sound too difficult at first, so I took her up on it."

"A wager, huh?" he asked, cocking an eyebrow. "Sounds interesting." He sat up and rested an elbow on his bent knee, bringing himself closer to her.

The resonance of his deep voice made Laurel's pulse pound furiously. She found his nearness distracting. He was utterly perfect, she thought. Everything about this man was ideal: he was kind and understanding, easy to talk to, and funny. Add to that his dark good looks, his muscular body, his rich, sensuous voice, and you came up with absolute perfection. Her chest rose and fell at an abnormal rate, then she started as if waking from a trance, realizing she had stopped talking and had been brazenly staring at him. The empty wineglass in her hand caught her attention and she frowned.

Picking up the pitcher of iced tea she had packed, she sloshed some into her glass. She clutched it with both hands and gulped down a swallow. The icy bitterness of the tea calmed her a little. She took another sip, trying frantically to remember what they had been discussing.

The bet! she remembered. He had said Ginny's

bet sounded interesting. She cleared her throat with a little cough before speaking.

"Not very interesting, really," she told him. "I want Ginny to be a responsible person. And, Lord knows, she equates responsibility with stagnation. So I have to show her that it's possible that a person can be responsible and also have a good time. She says if I go out on some dates, with men, of course..."

"Of course," Michael interjected.

Hot color mantled her cheeks when she realized what she'd said. The man doesn't need to know that going out on dates "with men" wasn't something she often did!

"Anyway, if I go out...then she'll go to college." Laurel lifted a finger and tilted her head. "No, wait. She said she'll *think* about going to college."

"Sounds kind of one-sided to me." Michael stretched out on his side, resting his head on his hand.

As he moved, Laurel couldn't stop her eyes from traveling down his long, muscular frame. She held her breath and quickly looked up, riveting her gaze to his face.

"Well, if I can change her attitude even a little bit, it'll be worth it." She picked up an apple, offering it to Michael before crunching into its juicy flesh.

A dribble of apple juice trickled down her chin. Michael could almost taste the tangy sweetness of the Macintosh on her soft lips. But he was too bothered by the sound of this wager business to act on the urge. It bothered him to think of her out on the town having a good time with a different man every night. What did "having a good time" mean, anyway? Maybe he should suggest one or two of his friends as able dates. At least he'd know whom she was out with. But that idea nettled him even more.

"But," he heard her say after she swiped her fingers across her mouth, "I'm a little worried about exactly how far she expects me to take this."

"Listen," he said. Not wanting her to sense the irritation he himself couldn't understand, he lounged back against the tree trunk, hoping he looked cool and collected. "I don't know if this little wager you have with Ginny is such a good idea."

Frowning, Laurel swallowed a bite of apple and waited for him to elaborate.

"You don't seem like you're the kind of person who can handle a casual affair." The words hadn't come out quite as he'd intended, and watching her take a tiny bite of apple and chew it slowly, he was unable to read her expression.

"Your sister can't expect you to compromise your morals for her sake." Another rash statement, he thought. This one made Laurel stop chewing and lower her gaze. Good Lord, now he'd embarrassed her.

"What I mean is, Ginny has to learn to appreciate you for what you are."

She raised her head. Her green eyes connected with his, making him wonder what she was thinking.

"Besides, you can't give in to her every whim." Seeing a storm brewing in her the sudden tenseness around her eyes and mouth, he thought he should have quit while he was ahead.

"And you think that's what I'm doing?" She gestured toward him with the half-eaten apple.

The sharpness in her question sparked his irritation to an explosive level.

"Well, you can't teach the girl responsibility if you're off Lord knows where with Lord knows who doing Lord knows what!" He returned her glare until she turned her gaze toward the horizon.

Was he right? Laurel asked herself. Was she compromising her morals for her sister? Was she giving Ginny's every frivolous impulse top priority? Laurel felt entangled as the maze of questions twisted around in her head.

For goodness' sake, she was only planning on a date or two! He made it sound...dirty. But he was right about her giving in to Ginny. It was something she'd always done. Wasn't that how you showed someone that you loved them? Maybe not. Not this time, anyway.

Michael was right, Laurel finally realized. She couldn't do this. She would have to find another way.

The annoyance Michael had felt left him as quickly as it had come. He had no idea what it was that had pushed him to question her reasoning as he had, but he'd succeeded in telling this woman, whom he hardly knew, that she was frigid, loose and weak of character all in a span of about thirty seconds. He was baffled by his behavior. But the drive he'd felt to dissuade Laurel from her plans was insistent and stronger than he could resist.

"Listen, Laurel, I'm really sorry..." he began, but her huge sigh caused him to stop.

"It's all right," she told him.

He was surprised to see that her eyes had gone

soft, that her lips, still moist with juice from the apple, curled at corners in a small smile.

"Don't apologize. You're right. You're right about everything. The bet was a bad idea and I'll talk to Ginny about it as soon as I get back to the cabin."

Relief flooded through his body. Michael didn't care whether he was right or not. He was just awfully glad she wasn't going through with the crazy wager.

~ ~ ~

"You blew it, didn't you?" Ginny twisted her mouth snidely.

Panic wrapped around Laurel's chest, making it extremely hard to breathe. She looked at her sister's expression and tried to remain calm. Having thought long and hard, she was sure she had come up with the perfect speech to tell Ginny that their bet was off. She had planned to say that it was foolish to play games with life and that that was something adults didn't do. She was going to explain that there was a right way to do things and there was a wrong way.

But Laurel hadn't planned on her sister's having one of her wild mood swings. Having heard the front door slam, then seeing Ginny's tight expression and hunched shoulders when she stomped into the kitchen, Laurel knew something was wrong. But before she could find out what it was, Ginny had verbally attacked her.

"You don't have to say a word," Ginny said. "It's written all over your face."

Laurel stared down at the mug of cold tea that sat on the table in front of her. She wrapped her shaking hands around it and tried to think.

"Where's Eric?" she asked, groping for an out. "Did you two have a fight?"

"I don't want to talk about him. He's such a wimp!" Ginny ground out contemptuously.

"If you had an argument, we should talk about it."

"Don't try to change the subject!" Ginny snapped. "I want to know why you can't even go on a simple picnic without messing everything up." She stood by the table, her fist planted on outthrust hip.

She had to calm her down, Laurel thought. Ginny wouldn't listen to a word she had to say until she was in a better state of mind. Then Laurel heard a panicked little voice inside her head whisper, *Lie*.

"Who said I messed anything up?" Laurel gave what she hoped was a soothing smile. "I had a terrific time today with Michael. The picnic was...very romantic."

That wasn't too much of a lie, she told herself. She did have a terrific time.

However, her smile wilted slightly under Ginny's dubious stare and she quickly decided to do a bit of elaborating.

"Michael's a great guy."

He is, he is! the little voice whispered.

"We talked. Got to know each other. We enjoyed a bottle of wine."

True, true, and true, the voice in her head intoned proudly.

"And he wants to take me out."

The little voice groaned.

Now where on earth had that come from?

When Michael had left this afternoon, they'd made no plans to see each other again.

"When?" Ginny asked, still unconvinced.

"When?" Laurel repeated. She swallowed, moistened her lips, and slid the mug a few inches away from her. She needed time to think. "Well, tonight, of course."

Goodness, it was really getting deep now.

"Tonight?" The look on Ginny's face brightened. It couldn't yet be called a smile, but it was no longer a frown, either.

"Yes. Yes, tonight. Soon, as a matter of fact. I have to go get ready." Laurel scooted back the wooden chair. She escaped to the bedroom and closed the door.

What was the matter with her? What had she done? What had happened to the idea of making Ginny appreciate her for who she was? She sat on the bed and tried to figure out where to go from here. She'd dug a hole for herself and now she needed to figure out how to get out of it.

"Where's he taking you?" Ginny's voice was muffled by the door.

"Um, just out to dinner, I think."

"You think? You don't know?"

"No, no. I know. We're going to dinner."

"Well, when will he be here? Do we have time to talk? I want to hear all about what happened on the picnic today."

Rubbing her fingers across her forehead, Laurel fretted. She hated lying. But she was in this now, and short of admitting everything to her sister right now...

That's it! She slapped her knee.

"I'm meeting him."

"Oh." Ginny's excitement took a sudden nosedive. "But I wanted the car,"

A frustrated sigh rushed past her lips before she could stop it.

"*What?*"

"Nothing. Er, that's okay, sweetie. You can have the car. I'll walk to Michael's place." She dug down into the drawer looking for a warm sweater. *I'll just take a long walk*, she reasoned. Ginny would never know. By the time she got back, Ginny would have gone out with her friends, and she would be in the clear.

She looked toward the ceiling and whispered, "If I get through this, I'll never lie again." After pulling on a thick sweater, she reached for the doorknob.

"You're going out looking like that? You only changed your sweater."

"Well," Laurel said, gazing down at her cords and worn sneakers. "You see, we're not going out. Yes, uh, he's cooking dinner for me."

The hole was just getting deeper.

"Wow! He cooks?"

"I guess so. Yeah." Laurel nodded nervously. Her glance darted to the window to see a brisk breeze tossing the treetops. It would be chilly while she was out, but she should be warm enough as long as she could get back to the cabin before dark.

"You said you needed the car. What are your plans? When are you leaving?"

"Well, I'm not going out, actually. At least, not for long. I'm going to pick up the girls and a pizza. And, since you'll be at Michael's, I don't have to ask if you mind if we come back here to hang out."

"Oh." For a split second Laurel was caught with her defenses down, and that one tiny word held all the disappointment and frustration she was feeling.

"That's okay, isn't it?" Ginny asked, a puzzled furrow in her brow.

"Sure, why wouldn't it be okay?" Laurel shrugged one shoulder exaggeratedly high.

Ginny cocked an eyebrow. "You do have a date tonight, don't you?"

"Of course I do!" Laurel snapped, not sure if she was angry at Ginny for pushing her into this stupid bet or herself for getting in deeper with blatant lies. But she would much rather face a room full of dark, handsome forest rangers right now than one moody teenager.

"Good!" Ginny said with a tight jerk of her head. Then she turned and went back into the kitchen.

Laurel took advantage of her sister's absence by slipping a paperback book off a nearby shelf and quickly stuffing it under her bulky sweater. There was no telling how long she'd have to stay out now.

"Here!"

Laurel spun around to see Ginny thrusting the bottle of wine at her that Michael had brought on the picnic.

"Take this with you. There's not much left, but

you can enjoy a glass with your dinner." She snickered as she added, "It would be impolite to go empty-handed."

When Laurel reached out to take the bottle the book slipped. She jerked her arm down, trapping it against her stomach.

"Are you okay?" Ginny asked.

"Fine, just fine," Laurel said, snatching the bottle. "I gotta go. Have a good time."

She was out the door and down the porch steps in a flash.

The things I do for that girl! she fumed. She kicked her way through the fallen leaves along the path.

"Where the heck am I going?" She stopped short, turning her face skyward. All she heard in answer was the sound of the trees tapping their objection as the wind plucked at their leaves, sending them floating to the ground around her. Closing her eyes, she sighed and let the quiet peace of the forest fill her.

Okay, she asked herself, where *are* you going? Memories of the lovely golden oak tree she and Michael had lunched under propelled her along the path toward the meadow. But it wasn't long before the sun dropped behind the mountain, twilight changing the bright and serenely inviting forest to a duskily shadowed wilderness.

She had three choices, she thought. She could go back and confess everything to Ginny; wander around helplessly lost in the forest; or go to Michael's house. Not hesitating more than an instant, she veered right when she came to the path that he'd pointed out earlier.

"Hello there, I just happened to be in the neighborhood," she practiced, wondering what he'd say when she showed up on his doorstep.

He probably won't be happy about what I've done, she thought. *Hell, I'm not happy about what I've done! But I'd rather face his disapproval than another teenage tirade.*

The path opened up at the back of the cabin. She stepped up on the rear porch and took a deep breath.

"Well, here goes nothing."

Repeating her unanswered knock, she stepped over and peered into the kitchen window. Except for a dim light that shone over the sink, it was dark inside. Laurel snapped her fingers smartly.

"That's right, he's a judge tonight," she whispered, remembering him telling her of the Autumn Glory Queen contest during their hike up to the meadow. "Well, Laurel, what do you do now?"

Brushing a few leaves away, she settled herself as comfortably as possible on the small back porch. The rough-hewn logs that made up the outside walls of the cabin were hard against her back. She ignored them as best she could. Hunger pangs grumbled in her stomach, and she ignored them, too, sticking her nose in the book she'd brought.

But dusk soon turned to darkness, making it impossible to read, so she set the book aside. The wind died completely, leaving the chilly night air disturbingly quiet. She pulled the sleeves of her sweater down over her hands and shivered.

The trees on the edge of the woods were barely visible, the blackness behind them haunting. An eerie creaking of wood and a fitful rustling in the bushes filtered out of the blackness. It could be anything; a deer, a raccoon, a squirrel...a bear.

"There's nothing out there. Nothing!" Hugging her knees to her, she couldn't tell if her shaking was from cold or fright.

Grasping the half-filled bottle of wine that Ginny had forced her to bring, she took a hefty gulp, then another. When a muffled crack was followed by a thump, she stared round-eyed into the ebony night. Something stirred in the underbrush. She couldn't see a thing, but her mind conjured up the vivid image of a hulking brown grizzly thrashing around, sniffing for its dinner...which could, as likely as not, very well be her.

Stop it! It's an opossum or a raccoon or a skunk. Wine trickled over her tongue and warmed her throat as she took another long draw. "Or a werewolf," she added right out loud, suddenly chuckling at her own fear. The muscles in her limbs slowly relaxed and tingled with heated weight.

"Let 'im come. I'll whack 'im in the head," she muttered, taking another sip from the bottle. Giggling, she thought of her first meeting with Michael and wondered if she really would have hit him.

"Of course I wouldn't have," she muttered. Sliding her legs up close to her body, she hugged them to her with one arm. The other kept lifting the bottle of liquid warmth to her mouth.

"What if he doesn't come home?" she wondered aloud. Imagining him with some gorgeous woman was easy. Would he hold her like he held me on the dance floor last night? The memory of his kiss rushed over her like a powerful wave. He'd made her feel things she'd never felt before. Her senses had tingled with heightened awareness, and a deep-seated hunger had rumbled inside her, a hunger she knew couldn't be satiated by food. A tiny groan escaped her lips as she rested her head in her knees.

What would happen when he came home? How was she ever going to explain this to him? He expected you to talk to Ginny about the meaning of responsible adult behavior, a small voice nagged her, not make up some fantasy date! Her shoulders sagged with a heaving sigh.

"He will never understand."

"Laurel?"

Smiling up at a slightly blurred Michael, she slowly blinked, wondering if her mind was conjuring up her fantasy. If her imagination was the culprit, it couldn't have done a better job! The dark suit he wore accentuated his well- proportioned body. He looked good enough to eat! Then she wondered if she'd merely thought the words or spoke them. She leaned her head back against the wall, hoping to stop his image from wavering.

"Are you okay?" His eyes were soft with concern.

"I am now." She grinned stupidly. "How did you find me?"

"I heard you talking. What are you doing here?" He sat on the step near her, his hand gently surrounding her ankle. Before she could answer, he asked, "Is it Ginny?"

She nodded. Watching him pick up the wine bottle, she heard a tiny bit slosh in the bottom. He questioned her with a glance, a smile tickling the corner of his mouth.

"I was cold," she explained.

"Let's go inside. I'll start a fire and fix you something hot to drink."

"Wait. Wait, Michael," she said, scooting over beside him. The sudden movement made her head swim and she put a hand on his solid shoulder for support. "Can we talk first?"

"But you're cold. Come on—"

"No, no. I'm toasty warm. I want to talk. I need to."

"Okay," he nodded. "There's a problem with Ginny?"

"More like a dilemma," she muttered. "But I don't want to talk about her." She wrinkled her nose and waved a hand through the air, wanting to push the subject aside. "I want to talk about me."

"You?" He tried hard to keep the amusement from his voice.

"Today you said I couldn't have an affair—"

"I said I thought you weren't that kind of person," he corrected. "You couldn't handle that kind of thing."

"I want to know why not."

"Well," he said, unable to control his lopsided grin. "Let's just call it an educated guess."

Michael stared into her glazed eyes. Her body slowly swayed away from him and she gave a tiny jerk to balance herself. He was more than a little surprised at finding her here. Something pretty serious must have happened to make her sit here alone in the dark.

He inhaled sharply, her weight pressing into him as she slid onto his lap. He felt her fingers lace behind his neck. She rocked backward and he steadied her; one hand spread across her stomach, the other on the small of her back.

"I think I can do it, Michael," she whispered.

Her wine-sweetened breath passed lightly over his face. His heart thumped wildly. The muscles in his stomach grew painfully taut. Her soft, parted lips silently called his name, and an urgent need to answer welled up in him. But he couldn't. Doing so wouldn't be right.

Although he'd known Laurel only a short time, he was sure this behavior was not part of her character. Something else motivated her actions, and he was determined to find out what it was.

"I take it your talk with Ginny didn't go well?"

"I said I didn't want to talk about her."

"And you feel you still need to prove something?" he pressed.

"Shh." Kissing the frown from his brow, she said, "I know I can do it. And you can help me."

"Wait." Lifting a hand, he gave a gentle tug on her arm.

"Kiss me, Michael."

She lowered her lips to his. Her mouth was warm and sweet, as he knew she would be. Desire overwhelmed him. Closing his eyes, he ran his tongue lightly across her silky skin. Helplessly, he deepened the kiss, wanting to taste her sweetness. She opened herself to him, eager for his exploration.

The fabric of her sweater was like velvet as he slid his hand around to rest on her waist, his thumb caressing the soft swell of her breast.

The kisses he planted along her jaw made her arch her back and offer him her neck. He kissed it, feeling the blood pulse rapidly through her veins. Her fingers wove through his hair, drawing his head backward, and she once more pressed her mouth to his.

He drew her closer and ran his hand over her hip and down along her outer thigh, then closer to the heat that was beckoning him. Laurel gasped at his intimate touch, and he quickly removed his hand from where he'd tucked it between her corduroy-clad thighs.

"Please," she moaned.

"Laurel." Taking a deep breath, he leaned back against the cabin, away from her, in an attempt to control the desire roaring inside him.

"You don't want me?" Laurel asked, drunkenly hurt but seeming somehow relieved.

She untangled her fingers from his hair and swayed away from him. He put both hands around her waist to steady her, and when she laid her head on his shoulder, he took the opportunity to slide her down his legs a bit. If he hadn't, he was sure she would notice his body's response to their kiss.

Wisps of her hair tickled his jaw as she buried her face in his neck. He smoothed it back, liking the silky feel against his hand. She was sweet-scented, and he filled his lungs with her fragrance. He felt her chest rise and fall as a tiny sigh escaped her lips.

"You make me feel so good, so safe," she murmured against his skin. He closed his eyes, fighting the tingle that coursed along his spine, the desire that curled in the pit of his belly, and knew she was anything but safe.

"Laurel, listen to me." He spoke softly, almost in a whisper. "I don't know what happened between you and Ginny tonight. I don't know what made you come here. Or what it was that made you drink the rest of that bottle of wine." He stopped and stroked her hair for a moment before continuing. "But I do know that what happened between us just now wouldn't have happened if you weren't...if you hadn't been drinking.

"There's no reason to be embarrassed or anything," he added. "And if you want to talk about your problem with Ginny, I'm still here to listen." He stopped, waiting for her response.

"Laurel?" He looked up at the bright, twinkling stars and listened to her soft, even breathing, the only sound in the still night air.

Chapter Five

"Laurel?"

Contentment washed over her as she woke to the husky male whisper. Wanting nothing but to slip back into her blissful slumber, she sighed.

"Come on, now. Wake up."

With her head pressed against his chest, Michael's voice was a soft rumble in her ear. He brushed back a strand of her hair, his fingers warming a trail across her cheek.

"We've been sitting here long enough. It's time to go in."

"In?" It took a laborious effort to open her eyes. Feeling disoriented, she sat up and rubbed lightly at her eyes. She was in the cab of Michael's truck, parked outside Jim's cabin. "How did I get here?" she asked.

"I carried you to my truck. Then I drove here." His mouth split with a grin as he teased, "You certainly couldn't stay at my house all night, now, could you?"

"You're right, I couldn't do that," she feebly agreed, but she was sure he hadn't heard as he was already out of the truck and walking around to open her door.

"Come on," he coaxed. "You need to get to bed."

It wasn't until she had stepped onto the porch that she remembered the way she had acted earlier, practically throwing herself at him.

"Oh, Michael." Embarrassment flooded her and she clamped a hand over her mouth.

"What?" he asked, alarmed. "What is it?"

Tilting her head, she gazed at the night sky. Gleaming stars winked and sparkled, unnoticed by Laurel in her shame. Dropping her arms to her sides, her shoulders sagged. A rueful twist tightened her lips before she spoke.

"I'm not even going to bother to apologize for my behavior." She frowned, fixing him with a steely stare. "You'll just have to take my word for it when I tell you that the Laurel Morgan you've seen tonight is not the real Laurel Morgan. I'm not a drinker. But then, I guess you figured that out."

"What worries me," Michael said, leaning his shoulder against the porch post, "is the reason that it happened."

"Ginny." Laurel couldn't quite keep her frustration hidden as she sighed her sister's name. "If there's one thing I've learned in the last three days, it's that I can't go on trying to be Ginny's mother." Shrugging her shoulders, she shook her head as she continued, "I mean, I don't know how to handle her anymore. One minute she's sweet as pie, then the next she's snippy, rebellious and hateful."

"I've heard of that. I think it's called adolescence," Michael teased.

Her frown softened at his good-natured razzing.

"Yes, I guess you're right. But, the funny thing is, I don't remember ever being like that."

"None of us do," he chuckled. "Don't worry so much." He took a step toward her. "I have a feeling things will work out just fine."

She looked into his eyes, wishing she knew what he was thinking.

"You get to bed," he said gently. Michael planted a quick kiss on the tip of her nose and whispered, "And remember what I said. Don't worry."

He stared at her, and for a split second his eyes lit with a mischievous gleam. "It's all going to work out."

Then he turned to jog down the stone steps, failing to notice the puzzled expression on Laurel's face as she wondered what he was up to.

~ ~ ~

"Wake up, sleepy head!" Ginny hopped onto the bed, tugging at the quilt that was tightly tucked around her older sister.

"Ginny, please," Laurel groaned, "stop bouncing. And leave me alone. I came in late." She tried to pull the blanket back over her shoulders.

"I know! You two sat out in that truck for over an hour!"

Laurel's eyes popped open.

Ginny laughed.

Struggling to sit up, Laurel thought through all the implications of that sentence. She had slept, cuddled against Michael's chest, for over an hour? And he just sat there and watched her? Her hands unconsciously clutched at the blanket as her whole body broke out into a sweat.

"You're blushing!" Ginny exclaimed. "Don't be embarrassed. I didn't see anything." She wrinkled her nose impishly. "But didn't you tell me that you were too old to make out?"

"Go away!" Laurel bellowed. She needed time to think. "Go make a pot of coffee or something. I need to take a shower." She threw back the covers, forcing Ginny to jump off the bed.

"But I wanted you to tell me all about your date!"

"Later, Ginny, later. After I've dressed and had a cup of coffee."

"You'll tell me everything?"

"Yes, absolutely everything. But later!"

"Okay, okay!" Ginny left the room mumbling. "What a crab."

Sitting up on the edge of the bed, Laurel rubbed her hands lightly over her face. Why hadn't Michael awakened her when they first arrived at the cabin? It was a question she couldn't begin to answer. Then, a slow warmth gathered inside her as she imagined Michael holding her, watching her as she slept.

Pulling her fingers through her tousled hair, she heaved a sigh. Really, what must he think of her? Grabbing her robe, she stuffed her arms into it. Ginny wanted to know everything about her "date." Laurel shook her head. And that meant more fabrications! She couldn't possibly tell her the truth.

As she padded toward the bathroom, she whispered, "Boy, this is not going to be easy."

Laurel sat at the kitchen table cradling a mug of coffee between her hands. She'd showered and dressed in a cheery yellow sweater and matching print skirt that was at odds with her mood. While she was showering, she'd thought about what she should tell Ginny. Keeping it simple, she'd decided, would be the only way to handle it. The last thing she wanted was to find herself hopelessly lost in a twisted maze of lies that would probably snap the thin thread of respect Ginny had for her.

"Okay, so tell me. Tell me!" Ginny could hardly contain her excited curiosity.

"There's really not all that much to tell. I went to Michael's, I had a good time, and he brought me home."

"Well, that's a bit skimpy on the details." Ginny's eyes were wide with exasperation as she watched Laurel sip her coffee. "Okay, I can see we'll have to take this slow. Let's focus on the 'good time' part. Tell me about your good time."

"Ginny!" Laurel laughed nervously. "I had a good time, that's all!"

"You said he was going to cook for you. What'd he make?"

Laurel picked up the teaspoon that was lying on the table, studying its flowery pattern intently.

"I'll bet he broiled steaks," Ginny said.

"Um, yeah, steaks," Laurel lied, her eyes not leaving the spoon in her hand.

"Men always do steaks! They have no

imagination." Ginny rolled her eyes heavenward. "I'll bet he made a salad, too?"

"You've got it," Laurel said lightly. "Steaks and a salad."

"Anything else?"

"Oh, uh, a sauce for the steaks. He made mushroom sauce for the steaks."

"Candles?"

"Uh-huh." Laurel nodded.

"Wow! Sounds romantic," Ginny exclaimed. "How about dessert?"

She couldn't carry it on anymore, Laurel thought. "No," she said. "No dessert."

"Ooo..." Ginny's eyebrows wiggled expressively. "More time for kissing, huh?"

"That's none of your business." The spoon slipped from her fingers and clattered onto the tabletop.

"Touchy, aren't we?"

"Not touchy." Laurel shrugged. "I told you, I had a good time. That's all."

"Am I allowed to ask if you're seeing him again?"

"Yes, you're allowed to ask. And no, I don't think I'll be seeing Michael again." Laurel pushed away the tiny twist of regret that curled in her stomach. Michael couldn't possibly want to see her again, and she couldn't bring herself to lie to Ginny about another date. "You did say there were lots of fish in the sea. I thought I'd throw in my line and catch another one."

"Good grief!" Ginny laughed. "I've created a monster!"

Laurel was trying to think of some smug rejoinder when a knock at the front door made Ginny jump up from her chair.

"That's probably Sharon. We're going shopping this morning."

Laurel set her empty mug on the counter, too despondent to wash up the few dishes that were there. She couldn't believe she'd gotten through Ginny's inquisition without hanging herself.

I'll never, ever, lie again, she silently promised.

"Laurel, it's for you!" Ginny sang out the words.

Laurel stiffened, knowing, even before Ginny finished her last, drawn-out note that it was Michael at the door. Glancing heavenward, she mumbled a quick prayer.

"Lord, you really don't have to teach me a lesson. I just promised never to lie again."

She left the kitchen expecting to be caught in her own deceitful web but found herself immediately enveloped in a warm, tight bear hug. Michael's freshly shaved cheek was smooth against her own and his earthy cologne seemed as familiar to her as his touch. Caught off guard, she simply stood there, limp as a wet noodle. His quick, firm kiss shocked her even further and she stared at him, silent questions written all over her face, she was certain.

"Good morning," he whispered, a wicked gleam in his eyes.

"Morning," she croaked.

"I'm glad you're up and about. I came to take you girls out to breakfast."

"Oh." Laurel's throat was so dry she could hardly speak.

"Darn," Ginny said, snapping her fingers smartly. "Doesn't look like we'll be going fishing today, sis."

"You two going fishing?" Michael asked. "I didn't know you already had plans."

Laurel glared at her sister's innocent expression. "We do not have plans," she said.

"I do," Ginny said sweetly. "I'm going shopping, remember? You couldn't have forgotten that fast, Laurel. I just told you thirty seconds ago."

"Oh." Laurel cleared her throat.

"But you'll come?" Michael asked, catching hold of Laurel's hand.

"Sure," she replied, still not sure what he was up to. Her voice was tight with apprehension as she added, "I'd like that."

"Michael." Ginny's voice made them both turn toward her. "Laurel tells me you're one terrific cook."

Michael frowned in confusion, and Laurel quickly squeezed his hand to get his attention.

"Yes," Laurel said, trying to cover her panic. "I told her about the dinner you fixed for me last night." She spoke the words deliberately, hoping he'd catch on. Gripping his hand tighter, she added, "The steak. And the salad."

Before Michael could speak, Ginny piped in, "And she said the mushroom sauce was delicious."

Michael raised one eyebrow, staring down at Laurel. "My mushroom sauce was delicious, huh?"

He stared at Laurel for the length of a heartbeat, then two.

Taking the sudden wicked glimmer in his dark gaze as acquiescence, Laurel was flooded with relief.

"Absolutely delicious," she said, trying hard not to laugh at his crooked grin. She was so glad his back was to Ginny.

"Listen, could we go now? I'm starved!" She had to get out of the house before she burst into hysterics at this farce.

"Anytime you're ready," Michael said. "Better bring a jacket. It's chilly."

"You two have a good time," Ginny said.

When Laurel stepped out of the bedroom with her jacket, Michael placed a guiding hand on the small of her back. "Get a move on, woman."

"See ya later," Ginny called.

As they walked toward his truck, Michael exclaimed, "Mushroom sauce? I hate mushrooms!"

"I had to think fast," she said, laughing. "I couldn't tell her what really happened, now, could I?" She got into the truck and slammed the door, narrowing her eyes at him. "What's this all about, anyway? I thought maybe you were up to something last night, but the last thing I expected to see this morning was you on my doorstep."

"Well, I got to thinking last night." He started the engine and pulled out of the drive. "If Ginny was driving you to drink—" even though he said the words jokingly, Laurel felt her cheeks flame "—then you definitely needed my help."

"Your help?"

"From everything you've told me, you're obviously not comfortable with this dating idea." He kept his eyes on the road. "So I've decided...if you're in agreement, of course, that maybe I could help you. We could go out, make Ginny think you're fooling around a little, and, like magic, all your problems will be solved."

She shifted in the seat and stared at him. "You'd do that?"

"Why not?" He shrugged. "We residents of Oakland are a friendly, accommodating bunch."

Michael glanced over to see her reaction and was relieved to see her smile. He had stayed up half the night trying to figure out the best solution to their problem. He couldn't quite put his finger on when Laurel's worries had become his own, but in the brief time he'd spent with her, she'd stirred something deep inside him, something that made her happiness important to him.

What she needed right now, he'd decided, was a friend, an ally, even if she didn't know it herself. And he felt an overwhelming urge to be that friend.

"What are you grinning about?" Laurel asked.

"Oh, I was just congratulating myself on what a sly guy I am."

"Oh, yeah?" she mocked. "I want to know what happened to that big lecture you gave me yesterday?"

"Lecture?"

"Yeah, the one about teaching Ginny

responsibility, about her needing to appreciate me for who I am?"

"Well—"

"The one about not giving in to my little sister's every whim."

"But—"

"The one about not compromising my morals."

"Now, wait a minute!" He caught her hand in his and tugged at it, urging her closer to him. She slid along the seat until her shoulder was only inches from his. The warmth of his skin against hers heightened her senses.

"I said all of those things," he told her quietly, "before I realized exactly what it was we were up against. I mean, this thing is bigger than you and me. The way I figure it, we're going to have a long hard fight in front of us if we're going to beat this...this..."

"Teenager?" Laurel offered, laughter bubbling up inside her.

"Exactly!"

He rested their clasped hands on his muscled thigh. Laurel had to make a conscious effort to keep her breathing normal. She couldn't believe how rattled she was by his nearness.

Taking a deep breath, she released it slowly. *Calm down*, she chastened herself. *You should be on cloud nine! You don't have to go through this alone anymore. He's going to help you.*

Slowly, a fog of suspicion gathered in her head. Why was he doing this? What had made him decide to help her? What could he possibly gain? A stark answer formed in her brain: nothing.

Absolutely nothing.

Her spine went straight as she contemplated what his reason must be. Pity. He felt sorry for her! She scowled. Well, she could take care of herself. She didn't need anyone's sympathy.

"Michael, thanks for the thought. But I don't want you to feel that you need to do this. I mean, Ginny's *my* sister. This is *my* problem. And I can handle it." She tried to slip her hand from his, but he tightened his hold.

"I never said that you couldn't," he said solemnly. He glanced over at her. "Listen, I want to do this because I know what you're going through. I went through the same thing with Jim. And here it is almost three years later and he's just now getting himself straightened out."

His gaze returned to the curving country road. "If we work together, maybe we can keep Ginny's adolescent turmoil to a minimum."

He gave her slim fingers a squeeze. "How about it? Are we in this together?"

Laurel couldn't deny the relief coursing through her.

"When you put it like that, how can I refuse?"

Studying him, she gazed from his shining, silky hair, down his straight nose, over perfect, smooth lips, to his slightly indented chin and wondered why being close to him constantly made her come unglued, especially when he always seemed to be so calm and collected. He evoked extreme responses from her— anger and suspicion one minute, euphoria the next. She had to learn to control her responses to him, especially if they were going to work together to help Ginny.

"Come on, let's take a walk before we eat."

The suggestion shook Laurel out of her reverie. They had arrived on the outskirts of town. He had parked the truck, and Michael had spoken to her from where he stood at the open driver's side door. Sliding under the steering wheel, she stepped out and took his proffered hand.

"That's the old B&O Railroad Station. That building's over one hundred years old."

Her gaze, following the directing nod of his head, swept over the archaic brick structure.

She liked the warm, almost possessive way he propelled her across the street, with one strong hand planted firmly on the small of her back. As they stepped up onto the sidewalk, she was poignantly aware of the chill where his touch had been when his hand dropped to his side.

Listening to the deep timbre of Michael's voice pointing out one sight, then another, she strolled beside him down the main thoroughfare of the small town. She was startled when his grip locked around her elbow, twirling her around to face him.

"Step over here," he whispered, pulling her with him.

He moved to the window of a small boutique, his eyes roving the silver jewelry displayed there. "Give me a second to think."

"What's the matter? And why are we whispering?" She searched his frowning profile, then she lifted her head to glance around them.

But he caught her chin, guiding her attention back to him. His warm fingers traveled up her cheek, then under her hair to caress her neck. His expression softened as his dark eyes looked into hers. Bending down, he kissed her jaw tenderly, then he leaned into her and pushed his nose into her hair to inhale deeply.

Laurel felt her knees turn to rubber. Lifting one hand to his shoulder, she held on for dear life.

"Michael?" His name left her throat in a faint breathy whisper. His light kiss on her earlobe almost made her sigh.

"We're being watched," he explained. "Eric's across the street."

Laurel's eyes snapped open. Michael was putting on a show for Ginny's friend Eric. Of course, he was. Why else would he kiss her and touch her so intimately? Wow, he was good at this play acting thing. Ignoring the burning disappointment that filled her, she realized she was going to have to stay on her toes. Getting caught up in the moment was utterly foolish, she realized, locking her knees to stop their quaking.

What was wrong with her? If someone were witnessing her reaction to him, she might be accused of being in love with the man or something.

In *love*? That was ridiculous! She barely knew him.

When Michael straightened, they both swiveled their gazes across the street to see Eric watching them. The gangly teen lifted his hand in greeting and Michael did the same. Laurel stood there unable to move, needing the time to collect her wits.

"Do you think he'll see Ginny today?" Michael asked.

Laurel could only nod.

"But do you think he'll tell her what he saw?"

Again she nodded.

"That's great!" His mouth split into a wide smile and he clapped Laurel on the back. "Let's go have breakfast. I've worked up a hefty appetite."

He didn't notice Laurel's clenched jaw or her tight fists as she walked beside him.

When the waitress brought plates of fluffy scrambled eggs, bacon and steaming biscuits, Laurel's stomach growled. She and Michael had been discussing their friendly conspiracy.

After the way she'd felt when Michael had told her why he was kissing her, she thought she'd never be able to eat. But his affable banter on the way to the family diner where they now sat helped her nerves to calm and her tensed muscles to relax. She was relieved that he hadn't seemed to notice her profound reaction to his faked attentions.

His easy, jovial behavior after their little 'love scene' cemented a reminder in her brain that she wouldn't soon forget: Michael's conduct in front of the boutique had been one friend helping another, nothing more. And it was clear to her now just how important his friendship was to her. Too important to jeopardize by some silly adolescent crush, or whatever it was she was feeling. She had to make sure she kept her emotions in check around him. It was too easy to get caught up in the seeming romance they were trying to conjure. Much too easy.

"I think we'll be able to pull this thing off," Michael said between bites. "How about you?"

She nodded. Placing her fork down on the table, she leaned on her elbows, staring at him intently. "Michael, I really do appreciate this. I want you to know that."

"I do." His eyes crinkled with a warm smile.

He wiped his hands on a napkin and placed it on the table. "Oh, I forgot. I have to work a couple of nights this week, but that's no problem. You can come with me."

"To work?"

"I won't work you too hard," he said, grinning. "The campers staying in the park like to sit around a bonfire some evenings listening to legends and ghost stories."

"Sounds fun," she remarked. "You want me to build the fire? Or tell the stories?"

He threw his head back, laughing. "Neither," he said. "Just be there. You could listen if you like."

Michael could barely restrain his urge to reach across the table and take her hand as they talked. The feel of her soft skin against his had seemed so right.

As they'd toured the town earlier, he'd wanted to wrap his arm possessively around her slender shoulders. But he'd reminded himself that he had come to her as a friend, nothing more, and to take her in his arms would have been out of line.

But, seeing Eric across the street, he knew a great opportunity when he saw one, and his natural instincts had taken over. He could still feel the silkiness of her cheek against his own, see the supple creaminess of her neck, smell the perfume of her thick hair.

Wondering what exactly he'd gotten himself into, Michael gazed across at Laurel and smiled.

Chapter Six

"Did you ever in your life imagine that we'd be going on a double date?" Ginny nudged Laurel out of the way and peered into the bathroom mirror.

"Never," Laurel admitted, lowering the mascara wand she held in her hand.

"This is great, though." After examining her reflection intently, Ginny pulled a strand of hair down over one eye. "Don't you think so?"

"Yep, just great. But it'd be even better if you'd let me get ready," Laurel quipped.

Ginny sat down on the edge of the tub.

Having free reign of the mirror once again, Laurel finished coating her eyelashes, then quickly ran the brush through her softly curling hair.

"Do you think you're dressed up enough?" Ginny eyed her sister up and down. "I mean, this *is* a date."

Laurel set the brush on the countertop. She looked down at the warm wool sweater she wore and smoothed her palms on the thighs of her soft corduroys.

"Ginny, in case you haven't noticed, it's cold outside. And we're going to a parade." Glancing at Ginny's thin black stretch pants, Laurel remarked,

"You may be the epitome of fashion, but you're going to freeze your little buns off."

"Eric'll keep me warm."

Laurel's lips twisted dubiously and she shook her head.

The knock at the door made both girls' heads turn.

"You get it," Ginny whispered excitedly, hopping up and running to the mirror. "I want to make a grand entrance."

Laurel laughed to herself at Ginny's ebullience. There was nothing in the world that would make her want to be a teenager again. But, if she were honest, she'd have to admit to a fluttering in her own stomach. It wasn't the date that worried her. It was whether or not she and Michael could pull it off. Fooling Eric from afar was one thing, but putting one over on Ginny, up close and personal as this double 'date' would be, was going to be quite another. Laurel was afraid her sister would take one look at them and recognize the whole thing for the hoax it was.

But when she opened the door and saw Michael's crooked smile, her fear melted like a crusty autumn frost under the warmth of the morning sun. What replaced it was a strong current of awareness that made her heart pound and her breath catch in her throat.

She swallowed, then ran her tongue over her lips before returning his smile and inviting him in. After he stepped inside the cabin, she pushed at the door to close it and felt it hit something solid.

"Eric!" She pulled the door open wider. "I'm sorry! I didn't see you. Come in."

"We met in the drive."

Michael's rich voice floated over her, drawing her gaze. The golden flecks glinting in his sable eyes distressed her. Did he feel the magnetic pull between them? Or was he just laughing at her?

"And we're both a little early." Michael's tone held more than a hint of humor.

He was laughing! Well she'd show him that she could play, too.

"Eager, huh?" she asked silkily.

His eyes narrowed a fraction. "Oh, yeah."

Michael came close and she instinctively slid both her hands onto his broad chest. The fabric of his shirt couldn't hide the firm muscles beneath it. When he cupped her elbows in his palms and stared down at her, seemingly lost in a visual feast, her heart raced. Overwhelming emotions made it difficult for her to breathe.

Eric cleared his throat. Laurel blinked twice then heard his long, low whistle when Ginny entered the room.

While the teens were busy with their greeting and safely out of earshot, Laurel whispered to Michael, "You ever audition for Broadway?"

"Is that a compliment?"

"Let's just say I won't worry about Ginny seeing through you."

"I'm glad. That's what I'm here for—to put your mind at ease." Michael left her to join the others in exchanging quiet pleasantries. Laurel watched the smooth movements of his body as he sat down and felt drawn to follow.

Standing behind him, she placed her hands on his shoulders. He immediately reached up, without pausing in his conversation with Ginny, his strong fingers encircling her wrists. He tugged at them until she was forced to bend over, her face next to his.

He crossed his arms, holding on to her tightly, and his lips grazed her skin as he said, "I think we should get ready to go."

Laurel sucked in her breath and tensed the muscle that ran between her shoulder and neck as she made an effort to pull away from him.

"She's real ticklish," Ginny informed him, giggling.

Michael laughed, holding her captive long enough to kiss her cheek, and then released her. Standing, he stepped around the chair in time to watch Laurel shiver involuntarily and rub at her neck.

"You rat." Laurel glared at him halfheartedly but quickly joined in the laughter.

"Well, I'm ready." Ginny grabbed her coat.

"Do you think you'll be warm enough?" Eric asked.

"I'll be fine," Ginny assured him as she sauntered out the door.

Michael helped Laurel into her coat. Leaning down close to her ear again, he said, "I'd like to see you poured into a pair of those pants."

"Oh?" She gave him a mock-angry look.

"It's a compliment. Believe me."

"You're impossible. You know that, don't you?"

"I certainly do."

The sleepy little town of Oakland had been radically transformed. The usually quiet streets were filled with noisy people and ablaze with light. Banners flapped in the chilly evening breeze. People crowded along the sidewalks, searching for the best vantage point from which to view the parade. Children clutched colorful helium balloons in tight fists. One toddler cried as he watched his drift into the night sky.

Before they'd even found a spot to stop and watch, Michael called to a street vendor and bought a large bag of pink cotton candy. Ripping the plastic, he offered some to Laurel.

"When I was little," Ginny said, "Laurel would never let me eat that stuff. She told me it would rot my teeth."

"But what's a parade without cotton candy?" Michael pulled a tiny piece of the pink fluff from the bag and held it to Laurel's lips.

She opened her mouth, and in an intimate gesture, he placed the candy on her tongue. It melted on contact and Laurel swallowed.

"Tell yourself that it's good for you," Michael said, nudging her along the walkway. "This stuff is chock- full of vitamins, you know."

Laurel pursed her lips and shook her head as she reached for another taste. Laughing was so easy when she was with him.

They found a four-foot-high brick wall and decided to watch the parade from there. Michael's hands closed around her waist as he helped her onto it. Eric did the same for Ginny.

Michael hiked himself up beside Laurel, his thigh pressed tightly against hers. He wrapped his arm around her shoulder, and she felt warm and cozy. He was busy nuzzling her cheek with his nose when Eric pulled his attention away with something he said.

Laurel filled her lungs with crisp air and thought about how good it felt to be out in the crowd. She saw people every day when she was working in the shop back home, *lots* of people. But that was different. Customers expected to be waited on. Here she was just one of the spectators and could enjoy what was happening around her like everyone else.

She released a pent-up breath and her shoulders relaxed. It was wonderful to be away from the drudgery of working in the shop. The thought came from nowhere and stiffened her spine with guilt.

I love my work. But the thought came with too much hesitation for her to ignore. The shrill whistle of the band marshal had her shoving the disturbing thought aside. She'd analyze it tomorrow; tonight she had a parade to enjoy. Snuggling against Michael, she let the excitement wash over her. She couldn't remember the last time she'd been to a parade.

Laurel never knew fire equipment came in so many different colors. The usual red and white didn't surprise her, but yellow, pale green and light blue?

"It seems endless," Ginny commented.

"Fire stations from four states participate in this parade." Michael reached for Laurel's hand, covering her cold fingers with his warm palm. "Let me get you some cocoa."

"I'd love some."

Michael and Eric hopped off the wall and went for the hot drinks. Laurel looked over at Ginny, whose teeth had begun to chatter.

"I hate to say I told you so."

"Then don't," Ginny snapped.

"Do you want to leave?"

"Maybe in a few minutes." Ginny's shoulders started to shiver.

"Do you want my coat?"

"No," Ginny said brusquely. "It'll make me look fat."

Laurel stared in disbelief. "I don't believe you!"

"Sometimes you have to give up comfort to look good."

Opening her mouth to tell Ginny just how stupid that sounded, Laurel shut it again as Michael and Eric returned.

She wrapped her hands around the white foam cup Michael offered her, its heat seeping into her chilled fingers. Smiling her thanks, she lifted the cup to sniff the chocolaty steam.

"It's delicious," she said after taking a sip. "Michael, we're going to have to go soon."

He nodded. "Ginny's doing a good imitation of an ice cube."

With all four cups of cocoa empty, Laurel suggested once again that they be on their way.

Getting through the crowd was not easy, and it took several minutes before they reached Laurel's car. Once there, Ginny planted herself in front of the driver's door.

"Give me the keys, Laurel," Ginny demanded. "I want to drive."

Laurel handed them over without argument, realizing her sister must be anxious to get the hottest blast from the heater.

"Thanks!" Slipping into the car, Ginny started the engine and flipped on the heater's fan. "I have a surprise for you," she said over the noise, looking at Laurel in the rear-view mirror.

"What?" Laurel's breath condensed to lacy vapor in the darkness.

"You'll see."

Frowning at her sister's teasing tone, Laurel looked over at Michael only to see him shrug. She folded her arms across her chest, her frown still in place.

Michael pulled her against him and wrapped his arms around her tightly.

"Would you relax?" he whispered against her hair. "It's not three against one here. I'm on your side, remember? And there's no surprise that you and I can't handle."

He was right. She was overreacting. A smile curved her lips and she leaned back against him. His arms nestled under her breasts and she rested her head on his shoulder. They were content to sit quietly, listening to the muffled voices in the front seat.

Ginny snapped the radio on, filling the interior of the car with a slow, bluesy rhythm. Laurel closed her eyes, letting the music wash over her.

Engulfed in Michael's warmth, Laurel felt every muscle in her body relax. The heady scent of his aftershave combined with the warm leather aroma of his jacket seemed to intoxicate her. She felt the steady rise and fall of his chest as he breathed. A dull ache slowly gathered inside her and she opened her eyes, looking up at Michael's jaw. Suppressing the strong desire to reach up and kiss it was easier than controlling the languorous smile that played on her lips.

She was so content in Michael's snug embrace that she was barely aware of just when the car stopped and the purring engine died. Out of the corner of her eye she saw Ginny slide across the seat toward Eric. Startled, Laurel jerked out of Michael's embrace to sit stiffly on the edge of her seat.

She was astonished that she hadn't even noticed when Ginny had turned off the main road. The car was parked on a narrow dirt trail. The headlights were off, and the parking lights threw a dim glow over the trees. Twisting around to look at Michael, she was further aggravated by his cocked eyebrow and the stupid grin planted firmly on his mouth.

"Ginny, may I speak to you?" This was no question; it was a command. Laurel slid toward the door, opening it as she spoke.

A sound of protest came from Ginny, but Laurel cut it off immediately.

"Now."

Ginny shuffled out of the car and shut the door. She stood with arms crossed, irritation plain in her stance.

"What are you doing?" Laurel hissed.

"What do you mean?" Confusion was plain on Ginny's brow.

"I mean, *what are you doing*?" Laurel planted a fist on her hip, anger increasing the volume of her words.

Ginny leaned against the car, her eyes narrowing with annoyance. "Do I have to spell it out for you?"

"There are four of us."

"So?"

"Ginny, you can't expect me to sit in there and watch you and Eric neck."

"I don't expect you to watch. I expect you and Michael to entertain yourselves!"

They stood glaring at each other for several moments.

"You are such a prude, Laurel."

But Laurel didn't budge.

"Ten minutes, Laurel. Can you survive ten minutes?" Ginny pulled at the door handle and slipped into the car.

The silent forest pressed in on her from both sides of the narrow dirt road. Laurel still stood there, unable to move. Fury made her jaw tense. She wasn't a randy teen, and the idea of fumbling around in the back seat did not appeal to her whatsoever. She was sure she would enjoy kissing Michael, being kissed by him. But that wasn't the point. This situation was too much. Wrestling in the back seat was above and beyond the call of duty.

The problem was solved as Michael stepped out of the car and came around it to face her. The suggestive smirk he'd given her earlier was gone, replaced by a look of soft understanding.

"You still think we can handle any surprise?" she asked, her voice low, unsure.

He nodded once.

She glanced past him into the darkness. "I can't believe this."

"What? That we can handle this? Or—" he covered her wrist with his big, warm hand "—that teenagers go parking?"

His teasing question didn't lift her mood. He pulled her away from the car, walking several feet to a towering pine.

"I must have missed something along the way. I mean, Ginny's doing things I never even thought about."

His eyebrows lifted. "You never went parking?" he quipped.

"Michael, I'm serious." Leaning against the rough bark of the tall pine, she slowly rolled a large brown cone under her foot as she continued. "Who had time for that? Not me. Up at six to fix breakfast, take care of Mom, open the shop, wait on customers— then, you know, closing time is dinnertime, and when that mess is over, Mom needs me again. Then Ginny— school, homework, drama club, dance lessons. God, it's endless."

Kicking the pinecone away from her, she looked up at Michael. "It sounds like I'm complaining. I'm not. I'm just wondering how in heaven's name I can help a normal teenager grow up when I was never a normal teenager myself."

"Look," he said. He knew she wasn't looking for an answer, that what she needed was some support, someone to tell her it was going to be all right. "You'll get through this. And it'll all pass."

"Promise?" The word dripped with skepticism.

"It may take four or five years...."

She groaned.

"Maybe longer."

She laughed. "You're supposed to be making me feel better."

"Well, some things you can never feel better about, and adolescence is one of them." He took a step closer to her, wrapping his arms around her waist. "Speaking of adolescents, there are two of them looking this way."

He leaned against her and gently kissed her lips. "Let's say I tutor you on the fine art of parking."

"Here?"

"Uh-uh." He bent his head and kissed the curve of her neck.

She swallowed, giddiness gathering in her chest. "But we're not in a car."

"We're close enough."

His breathy words against her ear didn't tickle this time. Instead they sent a delicious tingle all through her. His tiny nibbling kisses made her sigh. Kissing his way up her throat and along her jaw, he pressed his warm lips against hers. She felt woozy and weak, and she longed to wrap her arms around him.

He lifted his head when Ginny started the car and revved the engine.

Releasing a forceful breath, he caught it

midway with a grin. "Looks like your lesson's going to have to wait." He gave her a light kiss and, taking her hand, led the way to the car.

Disappointment descended on her. She would have loved to further her education.

~ ~ ~

"Well, what am I supposed to do while you're gone?" Ginny complained.

"I don't know. Call Eric. Or Sharon." Laurel pulled the brush through her hair.

"Can I go with you? I'll call Eric and we could all go together, like our last double date."

"No, Gin." The last thing Laurel wanted was another date with her sister. Playacting was a nerve-racking business. What she wanted, what she *needed*, was a nice, quiet, uncomplicated evening. "Michael's working. You can't invite yourself along. You probably wouldn't enjoy yourself anyway. We'll be sitting around a fire with strangers, roasting marshmallows and telling stories."

Ginny pouted. "You've been out with Michael three nights in a row. How late will you be?"

"I don't know." Laurel laughed at the question. "Why are you giving me the third degree?"

"I'm not." Ginny's chin jutted out. "It just doesn't look good, that's all."

"Doesn't look good?" Laurel couldn't believe her ears.

"No. And Dad wouldn't like it."

"Dad wouldn't like it?" Laurel repeated. "Let me ask you something, young lady." She was suddenly so irritated she didn't notice she'd lapsed into using her listen-to-me-I'm-your-mother voice. "Where was all this conscientious judgment when I was walking the floor waiting for you to come home, worried to death, hoping Mom and Dad didn't wake up?"

She threw the brush down and it skittered across the counter.

Hearing the wheels of Michael's truck crunch on the gravel drive, Laurel pushed past Ginny. She grabbed her coat.

"Don't you ask me what time I'll be in. I don't know." She yanked open the front door and turned back to Ginny. "But don't wait up for me!" Slamming the door, Laurel stomped down the steps.

The truck barely came to a stop before Laurel snatched the door open and climbed in beside Michael to sit in fuming silence.

"I sure hope it wasn't something I said."

In no mood for teasing, Laurel ignored him. The seatbelt strap gave her fits, but when she'd finally fastened it, she realized he hadn't yet put his truck into reverse.

Finally, he murmured, "My grandmother would be very disappointed."

"What?" She glanced over at him, thrown off guard.

"It was my grandmother's opinion that a gentleman called for his date at her door."

His silliness lightened her mood and she quickly found it contagious. "So your grandmother was an opinionated lady, huh?" She sighed and released the tension from her body. "It's her."

"Ah, the infamous baby sister." He nodded in understanding.

"She's in there sulking." Laurel shook her head. "You won't believe what she said. She wanted to come with us. She wanted to know how late I would be. She complained that I'd been out with you three nights in a row. She said Dad wouldn't like it."

"Wouldn't like what?"

"I'm not sure. I didn't give her much time to explain." She grinned. "What I did give her was a piece of my mind. Then I walked out."

"That's good."

"I thought so. It felt great."

Michael turned the truck around and pulled onto the main road.

"Well, I think it may be working."

Laurel was confused. "What do you mean?"

"The proverbial shoe is now on the other foot. Due to my extraordinary acting, Ginny believes that I'm lost in my lust for you. And you've done a beautiful job of making her see you enjoy it." He shrugged. "But then, what woman wouldn't?"

Laurel looked away, covering her face with one hand. "Give me a break," she muttered.

"Seriously, though, I think it'll be good for her to be the one worrying for a change. She may not understand it, or like it for that matter, but we're opening her eyes. We're helping her to see what it's like to be on the other side of things; to be the one who's worrying. And that's something to feel good about."

He steered the truck into a parking spot and turned off the engine.

"The thing for you to do," he said, placing his hand on her knee, "is forget all about it. Relax and have a good time."

The warm, almost possessive, pressure of his hand felt good. Delightful tingles radiated upward, and like a fast-growing vine, the hot shoots traveled toward the place where her pulse had now begun to pound. She shivered involuntarily.

He patted her knee. "There's no need to act tonight, no need to worry about who's watching."

That quick little pat and his confession of relief thoroughly snuffed out her budding desire. What replaced it was acute annoyance. She was irritated by the longing that flared up inside her at his slightest touch. And she was also testy about having to be reminded that this was all a game, a game Michael was glad not to have to play tonight.

Why did this keep happening, over and over? Why couldn't she control her emotions? Michael seemed to have no problem at all doing it. Looking up at the night sky, his words rang through her head: *let Ginny worry, we're opening her eyes, we're helping Ginny.*

Why did she keep forgetting the goal?

"Come on," Michael said, turning to walk toward the group of people gathering around a large bonfire.

Watching his lithe movements, she sighed and knew that she'd have to be content to take a time-out from game playing. The trouble was, she wasn't at all certain she was acting.

The whole evening was an emotional disaster. Laurel had to constantly fight the depression that threatened to engulf her.

It wasn't the people. The campers were friendly and convivial. And it wasn't the location. The bonfire crackled and hissed, and the stars glittered brightly overhead.

But Laurel was confused, and she sure wasn't having fun. She was baffled by Michael's attitude toward her. He ignored her most of the night, spending his time circulating from one group of visitors to the next, making sure everyone felt welcome and included.

Everyone, that is, except Laurel. The only time he'd spent with her had been after a young man had sat down next to her and started a conversation. Laurel glanced up to see Michael looming over them, silent, almost brooding. He had stood there, unmoving, until the young man made an awkward excuse and moved away. When she'd stood up to ask Michael if he was okay he'd turned and joined another group, leaving her even more bewildered than before.

He's working, she kept reminding herself. It's his job to entertain these people. But as she stared into the fire, she couldn't shrug off the feeling that he was avoiding her.

She looked up when she heard him ask everyone to find a comfortable spot. As people were finding their seats, he came over and sat down next to her.

"You warm enough?" he asked her.

She nodded and watched him turn his head to look over the group. Michael smoothed his palms together, and then he began to speak. He recounted a time when white settlers first moved into the area, when Indians roamed the land; a time when black bears were plentiful, so plentiful that a man could hunt and shoot five or more in a single day—a practice that, if done today, would extinguish the bears from the face of the earth in less than a week.

He told them of the river, the one so close to the mighty, eastward-flowing Potomac, but because it flows toward the Ohio, the native people referred to it as Youghiogheny, meaning, 'flowing in the contrary direction.'

The Europeans who settled in Western Maryland were hearty, hardworking people, and Michael recounted tales of half a dozen locals who had made a name for themselves in one way or another.

Her favorite story was the one about Negro Mountain and how it was named for a man who accompanied Colonel Cresap on an expedition. Nemesis, named for his great strength, was the only member of the party killed. An eerie silence fell over the group when Michael told them that legend said the black man had predicted his death beforehand.

Laurel's eyes darted over the solemn faces and came back to rest on Michael's profile. For nearly an hour he held the group spellbound. To break the tension, he slapped his thigh and announced that it was time to roast marshmallows. Chuckles and low, murmuring conversation floated into the night as people searched through the stacks of precut sticks for the perfect branch.

When Michael looked over at her, firelight danced in his eyes. Although he hadn't moved an inch, she somehow felt closer to him.

"So, what do you think?" he asked.

"You were wonderful. They loved it."

He stood and pulled her up in front of him.

"What about you?" His voice was like silk. "Did you love it?"

"I hung onto your every word." She reached up, smoothing one hand over his upper arm. Time seemed to slow down, and she yearned for him to lean over and kiss her. But his hands fell to his sides and he stepped away from her.

"If we're going to toast marshmallows," he said, "we'll need a couple of roasting sticks."

Watching him stalk off, she muttered, "Why did you *do* that?"

She shouldn't have touched him; she was only embarrassing them both. Sitting down again on the hard log, Laurel swore to herself to keep a tighter grip on herself.

Michael clenched his jaw so tight he feared it might snap in two. Why couldn't he keep his hands to himself?

He'd purposefully avoided her all evening. Except, of course, for the few seconds it took to stare down that Romeo who had come sniffing around bothering her.

He'd stayed away because he was working. He

shook his head ruefully. He had started out using that excuse, but that wasn't the real reason.

No acting tonight, he'd told her. And he'd kept his distance hoping she'd make a move toward him, give him some sign that she was interested in him as a man. But she hadn't. He scowled. So she wasn't.

Just help the woman out with her problem and leave it at that, he argued to himself. Frustration had him snatching two branches off the pile and scattering the rest into a mess he knew would have to be picked up before he left the gathering tonight. *And above all,* he railed, *control yourself!*

The ride home was uncomfortable, Laurel knew, for both of them. Conversation was forced, and the last half mile was spent in silence. When they pulled up in front of the cabin, no lights shone in the windows.

"You don't have to get out, Michael. Ginny's either out or sleeping. I have a key in hand." She dangled her key ring as proof. "I can make it from here." She moved to open the door, but his words stopped her.

"But you forgot about my grandmother."

"Your grandmother?" she asked, turning toward him.

"My grandmother," he repeated. "She'd be upset if I didn't—"

"Walk your date to the door," she finished, smiling at him in the dim light thrown by the dashboard. "I remember."

But the smile vanished from her face as they

walked toward the porch. She stopped before reaching the steps.

"Look, Michael." She stood in front of him, blocking his way. "We don't have to do this again—"

He cut her off by reaching out and dragging her to him. Wrapping his arms around her, he held on tightly, as if she might get away.

"Michael!" Her arms were pinned between them.

"Shh. The curtain's pulled back," he murmured. "Ginny's watching."

He lips descended on hers in one swift movement. Taken by surprise, she stood there, unresponsive. But the warm moist pressure of his mouth moving on hers was irresistible. She melted against him. Pulling her arms from where they were nestled, she hugged him to her.

All thoughts of holding back her desire vanished as she parted her lips, welcoming his deepening kiss. He held her tightly, but still it wasn't tight enough. Passion burned inside her like a hot flame and she moaned in unadulterated pleasure.

The sound died on her lips when he held her away from him. She looked up and clearly saw the question blazing in his eyes.

The fiery heat of embarrassment raged inside her and she looked away. How could she shame herself so deeply? How could her body betray her so completely?

Slamming a lid on her feelings, Laurel tried hard to compose herself, filling her mind with an icy calmness. Raising hooded eyes, she saw a deep frown creasing Michael's forehead.

"Well," she said in a soft, curt murmur, a tight smile firmly in place, "if that doesn't show her, I don't know what will."

His eyebrows drew even closer together and the air in his body left him in a rush. He dropped his hands to his sides and then stuffed them into the pockets of his trousers.

"I'll call you." He turned and walked away from her.

Laurel climbed up the stone steps, empty desolation roaming the cavern of her chest. *This can't go on*, she thought. She was bound to humiliate both of them before long.

She stopped before she unlocked the door, thoughts of Ginny crowding into her head. Would her sister still be angry and sulking, or would she giddily ask to know everything about tonight? Turning to look at the truck still sitting in the drive, Laurel sighed. Whatever mood her sister was in didn't matter. Laurel wasn't in the mood to deal with Ginny at all.

She pushed open the door halfheartedly, dreading the inevitable confrontation. Snapping on the light, she immediately heard Michael gun the engine and drive away.

The door closed softly behind her and she looked around the empty room. Surrounded by silence, she cocked her head in confusion when she identified the sound drifting down from the loft as the quiet snoring of her sleeping sister.

What was it that had made Michael think

Ginny had been watching them from the window? Maybe a curtain on one of the windows was askew.

But maybe...just maybe he'd seen nothing at all, she mused. A slow smile curled the corner of her mouth. Maybe he'd kissed her purely out of his own desire to do so. How delicious was *that* idea?

However, she laughed right out loud when she saw the arm of Ginny's jacket hanging over the back of the sofa, pressing against the window glass. So that was what he had seen! So much for that last delicious yet crazy notion.

Chapter Seven

Laurel paced back and forth across the floor. The quiet cabin held no defense as the rush of crowding thoughts converged in on her, thoughts of Michael and his overwhelming effect on her. After having spent every evening this week with him, Laurel was at her wit's end wondering how she could go on with this farce.

Fierce contemplation kept her unaware of how she prowled from room to room. How could she possibly spend any more time with him without looking utterly foolish, unable to control her mind or her body?

Her thoughts drifted back to his gentle parting kiss the night of the bonfire. The urgency with which she had clasped him to her had both surprised and shocked her. The flippant remark she'd made had been an off-the-cuff attempt to cover her brazen reaction to him—to his kiss. But had it been enough? She desperately hoped so; however, she had good reason to doubt.

Ever since that night there had been a whisper of change in Michael's attitude toward her. It started out with small things, a gentle caress or a searching look that lasted a moment too long to be called casual. What made it stranger still was that this behavior took place even when Ginny wasn't around to benefit. And as the glorious autumn days ripened, so, it seemed, did Michael's romantic attentiveness.

And in the last couple of days his intense affection toward her had become constant. Every moment she was with him was spent in nervous internal chaos. The caring she saw in his chocolaty eyes, the feel of his warm touch on her face, his light feathery kisses, all of these things left her senses screaming to respond to him.

It was clear that he remained 'in character' at all times now. Well, he certainly had the act down pat. So pat, in fact, that it was easy for her to forget he was performing, nearly effortless to overlook that it was all make-believe. She couldn't allow that to happen, though.

Michael's opinion had come to mean a lot to her. She would risk just about anything rather than appear to be a dim-witted idiot again.

"Guess where I've been!"

Laurel jumped, every muscle tensing at the sound of her sister's voice. "I didn't even hear you come in," she said. Ginny hung her coat on the rack by the front door.

"What's wrong?" Ginny asked.

"Nothing." The lies just seemed to roll off her tongue with ease these days. "Nothing at all. I was just going to make some tea."

"Well," Ginny said, following her into the kitchen, "are you going to guess?" She stood close to the sink as Laurel put water in the tea kettle and turned on the burner.

Finally, Ginny waved her hands in frustration. "Never mind. I can see you're not up to it, so I'll tell you." Sitting down at the table, Ginny lowered her voice conspiratorially. "I had a visit with Jim's fiancée."

"You met Darlene?"

"How did you know her name?" Ginny demanded. "When did you meet her?" She tilted her head and frowned. "And how come you didn't tell me?"

"Wait a minute, now. I never met her. I saw her once. At a distance. Michael told me about her." She told her sister about having seen Darlene the night of the dance but kept the details sketchy. "I was going to tell you it, but I forgot." Laurel slid into the chair opposite Ginny and eyed her curiously. "How did you meet her?"

"Eric and I got to talking about Jim. He told me about Darlene. Can you believe Jim's engaged? And he never said a word to us." Then she shook her head. "Anyway, I wanted to meet her, so Eric took me to her apartment early this morning."

"How did it go? What did you think?"

"She's nice, Laurel. Really nice. And she loves Jim. I mean, she *loves* Jim." The kettle whistled and Ginny got up to pour boiling water over the tea bags that Laurel had tucked into the ceramic mugs. "Why do you think Jim never told us about her? Or the wedding?" Her tone lowered. "Or the fact that he's going to be a daddy?"

"Michael seems to think Jim felt it might jeopardize his job." Laurel accepted the steaming mug, and after spooning sugar into it, she slowly swirled the liquid with a spoon.

"But that's silly."

"I think so, too. But Michael says that this is the longest Jim's ever held on to a job, that it means a lot to him. Makes sense, if you think about. Michael also told me that Jim intended to come back to marry Darlene and then take her back to Ocean City."

"Well, there's no need for that now." Ginny smiled smugly.

"Why? What do you mean?" Laurel stopped stirring her tea to look questioningly at her sister.

"Darlene wants to come home with us. And I don't think we should wait, Laurel. She wants to be with Jim when the baby comes. She says the baby's not due for another month, but if you ask me, she looks as though she could have it tomorrow."

"Darlene wants to leave with us?"

"Yes. That's okay, isn't it?"

"I can't see why it wouldn't be." But as Laurel said the words she wondered what Michael would think.

"I'm going to change," Ginny said.

But Laurel didn't even hear her go up to the loft, she was so wrapped up in her own thoughts. It was apparent Ginny wanted to go home. And Darlene wanted to come along. And from the sound of it they wanted to leave soon, at the earliest opportunity.

She'd been so worried about going out with Michael again. She'd brooded about it and mulled it over in her mind until she was sick. But now it would all be taken out of her hands if they left Western Maryland.

But how would Darlene's arrival affect her mom? The idea of having a baby around might deepen her depression, make her pine for the son she'd lost. Or a giggling baby might lift her spirits. And how would Jim feel about them bringing Darlene? Oh, but surely Jim would be more than pleased. He was planning to come back here to marry Darlene anyway. The two of them could just as easily marry in Ocean City as here.

And then there was Michael. How would he feel about all of this? Well, he had said he thought Jim and Darlene should be together, that they loved each other. Now they would be together.

But, she thought ruefully, more than anything else Michael would be relieved that this stupid game he and she were playing would be over, that he would no longer need to fritter away his time with her.

Deep inside Laurel felt a little relieved at the idea of leaving, too. But it was an odd sort of feeling. Empty and hollow.

"Laurel," Ginny said, waltzing down the steps, "I'm meeting Darlene for dinner. We're going to make plans about the trip home. I just need to drag the brush through my hair. You want to come along?"

"Thanks, but no." She shook her head. "Michael said he'd call."

"Michael, Michael, Michael!" Ginny scowled. "That's all you've been talking and thinking about. And you're sitting around waiting for him to call?" she asked, horrified. "God, Laurel, you don't wait around for a guy to call! What's the matter with you? Anybody'd think you were in love or something!"

Ginny disappeared into the bathroom. Laurel hadn't literally meant she was waiting for Michael to call. She had a lot on her mind and thought he might call while she was here. She shook her head. That didn't make sense. *Was* she waiting around for him? Her sister emerged, her long blond hair smooth and shiny.

"Look, Laurel, the purpose of this whole thing was for you to have a little fun. And I thought you were doing that. I admit, you looked a tiny bit stiff at times, but all in all, I thought you were doing a great job of having a good time."

Laurel stifled a sigh, remembering all the hard work she'd put in to making Ginny think she was having a good time in the midst of all this emotional turmoil play-acting caused her.

"I never for a minute meant for you to fall in love," Ginny continued. "You've only known the guy a week, for goodness' sake! And I could count on my fingers the number of times you've been out with him."

Ginny looked at Laurel piteously, shaking her head. "You just don't wait around for a guy to call."

"Okay, okay!" Laurel said. "I get the message."

"So, you're not in love?"

"Ginny." Incredulity widened her eyes.

Her sister's expression was unrelenting.

"No, I am not in love!" Laurel stated emphatically.

"And instead of hanging around here, you're coming with me?"

"Yes," Laurel replied. "I'm coming with you."

But even as she grabbed her coat and shrugged into it, she was shaking her head dubiously. She wasn't so sure a woman couldn't fall in love in just a handful of days with a man she'd met only a handful of times. Then she opened the front door and felt the warmth of the sun on her face, and she laughed out loud at the ridiculous notion. She *couldn't* be in love. It simply wasn't possible.

Michael drove up as she was locking the door of the cabin.

He greeted Laurel with a wide smile and a warm embrace, igniting flashes of fire in every part of her.

Trying to pull away from him, she found herself pinned to his side by the arm he held firmly around her shoulder.

"We were just on our way out, Michael." Although Ginny smiled, there was brashness in her tone.

"Yeah." But Laurel's agreement sounded limp even to her own ears.

"That's impossible. You see," he said, placing a tender kiss on Laurel's temple, "I have plans for you."

"Plans?" Laurel shied away from his kiss, fearing he might feel the blood pounding through her veins.

"Mm-hm. Plans that include soft music, candlelight...and solitude."

Donna Fasano

"But, Michael..." The rest of Laurel's sentence trailed off.

"It's okay, Laurel." Ginny laughed as she plucked the keys out of Laurel's hand. "You can't possibly miss out on something that sounds as good as that!"

"But what about Darlene?" Laurel questioned.

"Don't worry about it. I'll go myself. You can meet her another time." Ginny hurried down the porch steps and opened the car door, then turned back toward them.

"Hey, how about we meet back here for dessert, hot fudge sundaes? Say around eight-thirty? I'll stop at the store and pick up ice cream and all the toppings I can carry."

"Sounds good to me." Michael waved after Ginny. Turning to Laurel, he asked, "She knows about Darlene?"

"Apparently Eric introduced them."

Laurel could feel the desire emanating from his eyes, almost as though it were a tangible thing. She had thought herself out of the woods when it came to this game playing. With Ginny wanting to go home, Laurel had been convinced that she'd no longer need to be a pawn in this false romantic frolic.

Taking what she thought was a safe step away from Michael, she realized that even if she was a mile away from the man she wouldn't be safe enough. Just being near him, her body felt flushed with heat, ripe with anticipation. It became more and more unbearable each time she was near him as she found herself hungering for a look, the sound of his voice, the feel of his fingertips on her cheek.

She wouldn't, *couldn't*, put herself through it again.

"Look, Michael, I'm not feeling well." She closed her eyes, embarrassed at the lame excuse.

"Then—" closing the gap between them, he reached up and began to slowly massage her shoulders "—a nice quiet evening is just what you need."

His smooth voice was a balm to her nerves and she wanted nothing more than to relax into him, surrender herself to his gentle care.

No. She couldn't.

Her back stiffened. Planting her hands on top of his, she stilled their kneading motion.

"There's no need for you to take me to dinner. Ginny thinks—"

Michael placed a finger against her lips. "I'm not doing this for Ginny. I'm doing this for you. You've worked hard all week trying to convince Ginny that it's possible to be mature and responsible and at the same time have a free spirit. And I think you deserve a little pampering."

She looked at him questioningly.

"The table's set, the salad's in the fridge, the potatoes are baked, and the steaks are ready to be popped under the broiler."

"You cooked for me?"

"Everything except the mushroom sauce."

Her heart began to melt and she smiled.

Whoa, her conscience scolded. What about her

fear of being alone with him? Of controlling herself? Of embarrassing herself? But it was surprisingly easy to ignore the pesky questions. This most probably would be the last time she ever spent with Michael. Then it would be back to her busy, duty-laden life.

"What would you have done if I hadn't been here?" she asked.

He crossed his arms over his chest and sighed heavily. "Well, then, you see, the only part of my plan that would have panned out would have been the solitude. A lonely solitude."

Unwittingly, a tiny grin pulled at her lips. "In that case, I'd love to have dinner with you."

~ ~ ~

The fire crackling in the hearth combined with several well-placed candles filled the room with a golden glow. Laurel basked in Michael's easy company and the relaxing atmosphere. It seemed that he had turned off his romantic charm for this evening.

Was it her imagination or had she noticed that he was taking great pains not to touch her? He had let her hang up her own coat, claiming to want to see to dinner. And he'd also set her glass of wine on the table rather than handing it to her.

Well, she appreciated his platonic attitude and was content to sit and talk, person to person, friend to friend. She truly felt that he had become her friend this week. No one else but a friend would go to the lengths he had gone to help her with her problem.

He served dinner, and they ate in near silence. Maybe he sensed the end of her vacation looming in the not-too-distant future. Or maybe he simply couldn't think of anything to say.

"Can I get you anything else?"

Michael's question snapped her out of her contemplation.

"No, I'm filled to the brim. Thank you, though. Everything was delicious."

"Then, let's make ourselves more comfortable." He came around the table and pulled out her chair.

Again she noticed his hands had not come into contact with her. And when she followed him to the couch opposite the fireplace, he let her sit first and then settled himself well away from her.

"Tell me more about your family." Michael turned sideways, resting his elbow on the back of the couch. "I know we talked about them some when I took you to the meadow. But I'd like to know more."

"Well, you know Ginny."

"Yes, I know Ginny. And aside from being the tiniest bit spoiled, she's a great kid."

Laurel nodded. "I've come to the conclusion that I didn't do such a hot job of raising her."

"You did a fine job," Michael assured her. "Considering it wasn't your place to begin with. That should have been handled by your parents. I'm curious about why it wasn't."

She stared down into the crystal glass half-filled with rich, red burgundy. "There was a time when we were so happy, a real family. Dad, Mom, Brian, Ginny and me."

She looked into Michael's eyes and saw tenderness expressed there.

"When Brian died, it was as though a great black cloud descended on all of us. And it's been shadowing us ever since." Setting her wine down and grinning humorlessly, she said, "It isn't as though Ginny hasn't tried. God, how she's tried to break free."

"What happened?" he asked softly.

Her gaze left his face to stare unseeingly into the fire. Although Michael's query seemed vague, although he hadn't used her brother's name, Laurel knew he was asking about Brian's death.

Her voice dropped to a whisper. "He drowned." She was quiet a moment, then turned back toward Michael. "You know, it's been more than five years since he died. And even after all this time, those words still sound so unbelievable to me."

Michael's face relaxed with understanding, as though he wanted to absorb some of her pain.

"He'd gone out with a group of his friends. They'd been drinking. My brother went into the water after hearing a shout for help. That's what the others said, anyway.

"To this day I don't know if it was Brian's drunken state or the other boy's struggles that caused both of them to lose their lives. I'm sure I'll never know." She picked up her wine and, after sipping it, replaced the glass on the table. Sighing, she gazed at Michael's silent, concerned expression.

"I do know, though," she continued, "what Brian's death did to my family. My mother, who once was a happy, healthy, *amazing* woman, was transformed overnight. She turned into a ghost, Michael. And she's never recovered. You see, they'd had a fight that night, Brian and my mother. It was Brian's eighteenth birthday and Mom wanted him to celebrate with the family. She'd baked him a cake. And decorated it herself. She was so proud of it. Taking pictures..." Laurel closed her eyes, remembering. "I can still smell it. Two-layer lemon cake. His favorite."

Opening her eyes, she swallowed hard. "But, of course, he had other plans. He was a man; didn't want to be told what to do. Wanted to celebrate with his friends. They had a terrible argument. It was the first time I'd ever heard my brother yell at Mom." Her gut knotted as if the scene were happening all over again.

"Anyway, after the police showed up at the house to tell us about Brian, Mom went...she..." The rest of the memory was too unspeakable to describe. "An ambulance took her away that night. Ginny and I were told she needed to rest. I found out later that she'd had a complete breakdown. She was in a convalescent home for six weeks before she came home." Laurel gave a small, slow shake of her head. "She's never been the same."

Michael enveloped her hand in his.

"Mom sort of withdrew inside herself. She didn't want to deal with any of it." Blinking, Laurel was surprised to find her eyes moist, a tear slipping to the corner of her mouth. She raised a hand to dry her cheek, but Michael caught her fingers in his and gently wiped the tear away.

"And your dad?" he queried softly. "How did he react to all this?"

"He couldn't deal with Mom's silence. He

began to leave us more and more and stayed away longer on his buying trips."

"Which left you to run the business, deal with your mother and raise Ginny all on your own."

Hearing the words aloud and seeing Michael's sharp reaction to them, Laurel felt an enormous need to explain.

"Michael, people deal with the pain of death in different ways. Mom had hers and Dad had his. Who's to say which way is right or wrong? If it gets you through, that's all that matters." Her eyes pleaded for his approval. "Yes, I took care of my mother and Ginny. There was no one else to do it."

"No." He slowly nodded his head, the tension in him easing. "There was no one else to do it."

At some time during her story, he'd scooted closer. His long fingers slowly stroked up and down along her jaw. His arms wrapped her like a protective cloak and she felt soothed in his embrace. Resting her head on his arm felt like the most natural thing in the world for her to do.

"Life hasn't been fair to you." He traced the line of her cheekbone. "You've given up a lot for your family."

"Oh, but that's not true. I've been needed and I've been loved. How much more can you ask for?"

"Much more." He lightly fondled her earlobe. "You're beautiful," he murmured, his fingers blazing a trail down her throat.

Laurel lifted her head and, gazing into his eyes, saw dark sparks of desire. The calm, consoling mood between them suddenly shifted, and she wasn't quite sure how to stop it. Or, for that matter, if she wanted to.

When he pressed his lips to her forehead, she spread her hand flat against his chest. The pounding of his heartbeat quickened, and her own desire flared within her.

His eyes were darker now and he lowered his head to nibble at her ear. He kissed the line of downy hair behind it and a delicious shiver coursed through her. He kissed her mouth tenderly, gently, and liquid fire raced through her body. He nuzzled her neck with his kisses and little nips. She wanted to guide his lips back to hers, but it felt so good, so right, that she couldn't seem to lift her arms.

"I want you, Laurel," he whispered.

I want you, too. She wasn't sure if she had spoken the words aloud or not.

He covered her mouth with his once more and she returned his kiss with fervor. He pulled back, cupping her chin in his palm, and rubbed his thumb over her moist lips.

"Let me make you forget everything for a while." Nimbly working open at the buttons, he slipped his hand into her blouse to caress her breast. His lips brushed her throat and collarbone, then burned the creamy flesh of her breast. She lifted her hand to bury her fingers in his thick hair.

For a while...

For a while...

His words replayed themselves over in her mind, rousing her from the foggy depths of desire. He wanted her, desired her. She knew that. Could feel it in his kiss, in his touch. But the words tolling through her head told her that there was no possibility of a commitment from him.

It wasn't his fault. It was hers. She was the one who had conjured up this whole romantic scenario between them. She was also the one who had allowed him lose sight of their original goals. She should have spoken up the very first time his romantic behavior toward her was unwarranted. But she had relished his attention.

She relished it *now*. Yearned for it. She knew it would be easy to lose herself in this rage of longing that had caught them up, and that, if she made no move to stop him, he would make love to her. And if she let that happen, his touch, his scent, would be trapped forever in her memory.

But is that what she wanted?

Making love to him would be heaven on earth. But this moment would end. And all she'd have was a memory. Would that be enough? To live with a cold and lonely memory? A memory that would surely hound her all of her days? One that would cause her pain each time it was brought forth in her mind? Was it better to have something and then lose it and know the pain of that loss or remain blissfully ignorant from the very beginning?

"Michael, please stop." She tugged him away from her and saw his gaze thick with desire, his breathing as ragged as her own. Shaking her head, she said, "I don't want to do this."

He took a deep breath, then another, and dragged his fingers through his hair. "What is it?"

"Nothing." She fumbled with the fabric of her blouse and saw her fingers trembling as she fastened the buttons.

"Laurel," he said, catching her chin and raising her face so she'd look at him. "What's wrong?"

"Nothing's wrong. I just don't want to do this." Pulling herself from his grasp, she looked away, wanting to hide the truth from him. "And anyway, we're supposed to meet Ginny and Darlene."

He sat for a moment, quiet, frowning. Finally, he said, "Oh, I get it. Mother hen is back." He stood and strode over to the fireplace.

"What do you mean by that?" Laurel bristled.

"Nothing." Banking the fire, he replaced the screen and hung up the poker. "Come on, I'll take you home."

She'd done the right thing, she thought as they rode in silence toward the cabin. She was sure of it. Living with the memory of being touched, being loved physically, by Michael would be unbearably painful. It was better not to know the sweetness of it.

"Would you make my excuses? I don't think I'll come in." Michael's voice was low as he stopped the truck in front of the cabin.

"I understand." She got out, then spun around, saying his name just as he'd uttered hers.

Their eyes met and held.

What could she say? How could she make him understand the emotions roiling in her without looking like melodramatic teen with a crush? Finally, lifting her shoulder a fraction, she said, "It's not that I —"

"Laurel! Michael!" Ginny came bursting from the cabin, stopping at the top of the porch steps. "Please! I need you! It's Darlene!"

The desperation in her voice made both Laurel and Michael run for the front door.

Taking the stone steps in two strides, Michael was the first inside. When Laurel followed, she saw the young girl sitting on the sofa, her face pale and covered with a moist sheen of perspiration.

"It hurts," Darlene whispered, clutching Michael's hand tightly.

"You need to relax. Breathe slowly," he told her.

"She wouldn't let me call for help." Ginny was on the verge of tears. "I didn't know what to do."

"It's all right now. We'll help her," Laurel assured her sister. "Should I call an ambulance?" She directed her question at Michael.

"Yes."

"No!" Darlene was panting as the pain subsided. "I don't have insurance. I can't afford an ambulance."

"But...but," Laurel wasn't sure what to say.

"It's okay." Michael's tone remained measured and calm. "Plenty of pregnant women are driven to the hospital every day. I'll take you. My truck's outside."

"But it's nothing," Darlene insisted. "It's false labor. It'll pass. I've had it off and on all week."

"At least let us call your doctor." Laurel sat down next to Darlene. "He should know about this. He'll tell us what we should do."

After getting the doctor's name and number, she pulled out her cell and began dialing. The ringing on the other end of the line seemed incessant. Laurel watched Darlene closely. She saw Michael stuff pillows behind the girl's lower back in order to make her more comfortable. He sent Ginny after a cool cloth.

The only experience Laurel remembered having with childbirth was when her mother had been pregnant with Ginny, but because Laurel had been so young, all the pain and difficulty of it had gone unnoticed. The taut lines she now saw around Darlene's mouth were pulled even tighter as the girl was hit with another contraction. Instinctively Laurel knew there was nothing false about this labor.

"Come on, already," she whispered impatiently into the receiver. Why didn't someone answer? Finally, someone did, but Laurel was disappointed to find out it was only the doctor's answering service. She left her name and number and, before she hung up, told the operator that it was an emergency.

"But it's not!" Darlene wailed. "It's not time yet."

"There's no harm in letting the doctor have a look at you." Michael tried to placate her. "All we have to do is sit tight, relax and wait for the doctor to call back."

"I need to get up. I need to walk it off."

Laurel immediately made to help Darlene rise only to see Michael's glare.

"If her body's telling her to walk, then she

should walk," she snapped at him. "It's got to be better than sitting here waiting for another contraction."

Michael heaved a sigh, his shoulders rounding.

"You're right," he said, and he stood to help Darlene.

Laurel took hold of one elbow, Michael the other, as they pulled Darlene up off the couch. Immediately, the young woman gasped. Laurel looked down to see clear birthing fluid pooling on the floor at their feet.

Chapter Eight

Darlene's bottom lip quivered and she clamped it between her teeth. "But it's not time," she whispered, her eyes filling with tears.

"I'll get some towels," Ginny said.

"No, no. Don't bother with that now." Laurel was afraid to move from Darlene's side. "Get her coat, Gin."

"You want to come along?" Michael looked questioningly at Laurel.

She nodded. "We'll take my car."

Ginny bustled around gathering coats, purses and keys.

They stopped about midway between the cabin and the car as the girl bent over for a full minute, a wave of pain jolting through her.

Michael took the keys from Ginny. Laurel bundled Darlene into the back seat and crawled in after her.

Ginny climbed into the front beside Michael. Darlene's tears flowed unhindered.

"This can't be happening," she sniffed. "Jim wanted to be here." She blew her nose on a tissue Ginny handed her. "He wanted to be with me when the baby was born."

"You need to stay calm," Laurel reminded her.

"Take deep breaths." Reaching over, she took hold of Darlene's hand and rubbed it between hers.

It seemed to Laurel that they were creeping along on the winding, twisty road. She noticed Michael's tense silence as he drove.

"I'm awfully sorry." Darlene's pale face was covered with glossy perspiration. She swallowed and tried to smile.

"Hey, it's okay. You'll see, everything will be all right," Laurel assured her.

"You two haven't even met yet." Ginny turned around to face them. "Laurel, meet Darlene. Darlene, Laurel."

"You work with Jim. He likes working with you. He told me all about you."

I wish he'd told me about you, Laurel thought guiltily. I'd have sent him right home, trouble with Ginny or no trouble with Ginny. She squeezed Darlene's fingers reassuringly and realized what Jim had given up so that she could bring Ginny here. She smiled at Darlene. "Jim's a great guy."

"I think so," Darlene agreed. Then she clutched Laurel's hand, almost choking as she inhaled sharply. Panic and a healthy dose of fear widened her eyes.

"Michael," Laurel urged. "We need to hurry. Her contractions seem terribly strong."

"I'm going as fast as I can," he barked.

Laurel focused her attention on Darlene, who was panting.

"Slowly. Slowly. Breathe with me." Laurel inhaled deeply.

"Tell him—" Darlene gulped at the words "—tell him to take the valley road."

"We can't take the valley road!"

"What's the valley road?" Laurel asked.

"Shorter," Darlene panted. "Just ahead."

"Yes, it's shorter. But it's a dirt road, for God's sake! You'll be jostled all over that backseat. I won't take it. You're in enough pain as it is!"

"I can feel the baby coming." Darlene's voice broke with a sob.

Laurel leaned forward. "How much shorter is it?"

"Laurel, we can't take the valley road. It's full of potholes and it's overgrown in places. Every delinquent in town goes out there drinking, so it's littered with broken glass."

Seeing Darlene's stark white knuckles made Laurel repeat the question in a sharper tone. "How much shorter?"

"Quite a bit. But it's—"

Hearing Darlene groan, Laurel interrupted Michael. "Then I think you better take it because this baby's waiting for no one."

Michael let out a breathy curse. "Hold on, then," he advised them all as he turned onto the bumpy, narrow lane.

Sliding as far toward the door as she could, Laurel turned to Darlene. "I want you to lean against the door and bring your feet up onto the seat. Ginny, lock her door."

"Here," Ginny offered, "you might need these."

"You brought towels?" Laurel's voice held a note of surprise. "Great thinking!"

"But I wasn't," Ginny admitted lamely. "I also grabbed a bar of soap and the dental floss. Don't ask me what I thought we'd do with them."

"Here," Laurel said, tucking one of the towels under Darlene's hips. "This should be much more comfortable for you."

They were jostled back and forth as the car rolled along the dirt road. Loose rocks thumped against the bottom of the car, thrown up by the tires. The shocks bounced as they hit one hole after another.

"Michael, you can slow down." Darlene wiped her hand across her face. "I think it's over."

"Over?" Laurel and Ginny asked in unison.

Darlene nodded. "The pain's almost gone." She sighed, her breath catching on a relieved sob. "I was so scared."

"So was I." Ginny's head bobbed.

Of course, this wasn't over. They'd all been standing there when Darlene's water broke. This was merely the calm before the storm. But Laurel hesitated saying so for fear of upsetting this unexpected peace, no matter how fleeting it might turn out to be.

"Even so, Darlene," Michael said his words carefully measured, "I want to get you into town so the doctor can have a look at you."

Laurel leaned forward and touched his shoulder. "I agree."

"Well, that eases my mind," he muttered.

She snatched her hand away, resting her clenched fist in her lap.

The car lurched with a jarring thud as Michael hit an enormous hole, and when it bounced out, the tire exploded with a bang. He brought the car to a bumpy stop.

Michael swore softly. "I can't believe this. Sit tight. I'll have the tire changed in no time."

"Wait," Ginny said. Rummaging in the glove compartment, she pulled out a flashlight. "You'll need this."

The instant Michael opened his door, Laurel placed a hand over her mouth to stifle a small gasp. How was she going to tell him?

"Michael?" she called, swallowing nervously.

"It'll be safe," he informed her testily. "I'll brace the other tires with rocks."

He got out, and she called his name even as he stalked toward the back of the car. She heard him jiggling the key into the trunk lock.

"Are you sure you're okay?" Laurel asked Darlene. Seeing the girl nod, Laurel glanced at Ginny, "Stay with her."

The chill in the air nipped at her fingers and cheeks, and she rubbed her hands together, hurrying around to the rear of the car where Michael had the trunk lid open, a beam of light sweeping across the dark interior.

"Michael."

"Thanks, Laurel, but I don't need any help," he said without looking up. "Go back inside, where it's warm."

"I don't want to help."

He reared up, turning to face her, irritation plain on his face. "What is it, then?"

"It's not there."

"What?"

"The spare tire," she blurted. "It's on the car. The flat one, on the car."

He stood there staring at her as the news sunk in.

"You mean to tell me that you didn't get the other tire fixed?" His question was low, ominous.

"No, I'm not telling you that!" Anger sharpened her retort. "I took it, but the attendant was busy. I had to leave it there."

"But surely he lent you a spare."

She shook her head.

"What do you mean, no?"

Once again, she was left looking the idiot. But she wasn't embarrassed; she was plain mad. Her jaw was tight as she told him, "He didn't have one to fit my car."

The breeze that fluttered her hair seemed to have grown colder. As if the idea had entered their minds simultaneously, they both whipped out their cells.

No service, she read on the tiny black screen.

"I got nothing," he said, and then sighed as he flipped closed his phone and tucked it into his pocket. "So we're stuck out here with no way to call for help, a flat tire and no spare."

Laurel nodded, shrugging helplessly.

He sighed, rubbing his hand over the back of his neck.

"Okay," he said finally. "Here's what we're going to do. You get into the car and lock the doors. If you get cold, turn the engine on. There's plenty of gas."

"You going into town?"

"It's closer for me to run back and get the truck. I'll be back here in less than half an hour." He slammed the trunk's lid down and handed the keys to Laurel.

Hearing a weak tapping on the back window, they both turned to see Darlene laboring breathlessly.

Laurel opened the back door and stuck her head inside. "I thought you said everything was okay."

"Guess I lied." Darlene struggled to smile, but the furrow biting deeply into her brow and the fear plain in her gaze contorted the effort.

"The baby's coming," Ginny said.

"She's right. The baby's. Coming. Right now." Darlene let out a low, jagged whimper.

Pulling herself out of the car, Laurel turned frightened eyes toward Michael. "We're going to have a baby."

"Okay." He came up beside her and put a warm hand on her shoulder. "Don't worry. Together, we can do this."

She squared her shoulders, strengthened by his confidence.

"I'm going to brace her from behind," Michael stated. "It'll be much more comfortable for her than pushing against the door."

"But I can't..." Laurel's voice trembled.

"Of course you can," he assured her. "Just put on your catcher's mitt. Mother Nature will take care of everything else."

When Laurel leaned into the car again, Ginny was unlocking the back door. Michael wedged himself behind Darlene, one knee on the seat, one on the floorboard.

"Comfortable?" he asked Darlene, who only panted in reply. He looked up at Laurel. "This baby's coming awfully quick for a first delivery."

"Must run in my family," Darlene said breathlessly. "I remember...my mother telling me...I was born on our kitchen floor." She shifted on the seat. "But Mom said...I was a full term baby."

Everyone was still and silent as Darlene was hit by another wave of pain.

Laurel looked up at Michael nervously. "What now?"

"We wait."

Darlene huffed and puffed, strained and pushed, as the process intensified. Before long, the newborn lay cradled in Laurel's hands. The baby jerked in surprise when he sucked in his first breath.

"He's beautiful!" Laurel exclaimed, wrapping the infant in a towel and cleaning his eyes and ears with another.

"It's a boy?" Darlene asked. "Is he okay?"

"He looks perfect to me," Laurel assured her. She placed the swaddled baby in Darlene's arms. "Ten fingers, ten toes."

The stillness that settled over all of them

seemed a bit anticlimactic after the wonder they had just experienced. Then the baby let out a long raspy cry.

Ginny giggled at his solo. "He's going to be another Justin Bieber."

"Or Andrea Bocelli," Laurel said.

"Or Tim McGraw." Michael gently wiped Darlene's damp face with a tissue Ginny had given him.

"I do know that we need to tie off the cord," Laurel said. "I don't think we should cut it or anything, just tie it off. The fluid in the placenta will make him sick." She shrugged at Michael's questioning expression. "The miracle of public television."

Looking around the cramped back seat, he suggested, "How about a shoelace?"

"Here, use this," Ginny said, passing Laurel the container of dental floss.

Laurel smiled. "It's cleaner than a shoelace."

They all laughed, more with relief that the ordeal was over than at Laurel's joke.

Laurel slid her arms out of her coat and tucked it around mother and baby.

"It's cold in here," Ginny balled her hands under her chin.

"Slide over and start the car." Michael handed her the keys. "Turn the heater on." He eased himself out of the car, closed the door and walked a few steps to stretch his cramped muscles.

"Thank you, Laurel," Darlene said.

"You did all the work." Laurel patted the girl's hand.

"We just cheered you on," Ginny said.

Laurel looked from Ginny's beaming face to Darlene's tired one and marveled at the wondrous event they'd all experienced. She felt exhilarated. The miracle of life was just that—a miracle. But she knew it was not something she'd want to experience again. Not, that is, on a deserted dirt road in the middle of a forest. She personally would prefer a clean, well-equipped hospital.

She felt a pang of regret that Jim had missed the birth of his son. She sighed, pushing the thoughts away. This was not a time of regrets but a time of celebration, the celebration of new life!

Letting the euphoric smile take over her entire being, she shook her head in disbelief at what she'd taken part in. A baby had been born right before her eyes.

"I need to pull the knots out of my back muscles," Laurel said.

She left Darlene cooing to the baby, closed the car door and walked along the dirt lane. Never in her life had she felt so moved, so elated, as when that tiny infant had fallen into her hands. He was so helpless, his first scratchy cries almost making her weep.

Rubbing her lower back, she bent backward and stared up at the starry sky. She realized for the first time how lucky they were that the birth was uncomplicated. The implications of what could have happened forced a chill through her, and she whispered a quick prayer of thanks.

She sucked in her breath in awe as a long, sparking arch of a shooting star streaked across the night sky. She grinned and, not wasting a moment, wished for health and happiness for the new baby boy.

"You were great." Michael was beside her, brushing at a wisp of her silky hair.

"I was, wasn't I?" Laurel laughed. "But then, so were you, and so was Ginny, and most of all, so was Darlene."

"We were awfully lucky," he said seriously.

"I was thinking that myself."

Their gazes caught and held in the magnitude of the moment.

Michael rested his hands on her shoulders. "What happened between us this evening..."

She silenced him by placing a finger across his lips. "Don't," she pleaded. "I wanted you, too."

Understanding wrapped around them like a warm, woolen cloak. Their embrace was sweet, poignant. Laurel's heart was stirred with remorse. How could she have rationalized herself out of a few tender moments in his arms?

Cradling her face between his hands, he searched her eyes. "We need to talk."

She gave him a small smile of assent.

"I'm going for help." He kissed her lightly on the mouth. "Now, get inside the car and warm up. I won't be long."

He turned and jogged in the direction they had come.

"Michael, take the flashlight."

"I'll be all right," he called. "You may need it."

Be careful, she silently called as she watched him run down the rocky dirt lane. *You're carrying my heart.*

Laurel slid into the front seat with Ginny, wanting to give Darlene as much room as possible. Her deep, even breathing was a contrast to the baby's tiny sighs as mother and son slept.

"She was worn-out," Ginny said.

"How about you?"

"I'm okay. It was amazing, though, wasn't it?"

Laurel took a deep breath. "Amazing is a pretty good word to describe it."

"Darlene's the mother of that tiny little baby." Ginny whispered the words as if in awe. "Do you know that Darlene is less than a year older than I am?" Shaking her head, she looked at Laurel. "That could be me back there."

"Heaven forbid, Gin."

"But it could!" Ginny repeated.

Laurel saw Ginny's pensive expression, heard the severity of her words.

"What are you saying, honey?"

"Look at her. She's holding down a job, taking care of an apartment, and now she has a helpless baby that she's responsible for." Ginny exhaled with a sound of disgust. "I'm just a kid compared to her. If any of that would have happened to me, I wouldn't have been able to handle it."

"Now, you don't know that. People take what life tosses at them. Darlene's been thrown a curve ball and she's done a pretty good job of catching it, that's all."

Ginny looked out at the darkness. "I've missed every one that's come my way."

The lugubrious admission startled Laurel.

"Not every one," she quipped, trying to lighten Ginny's mood.

"Getting to know Darlene, the kind of person she is and the things she's done—it all makes me feel so...so young."

"But, honey, you *are* young," Laurel said. "And so's Darlene. You both have some growing up to do. She's tried to do it in too little time and you've tried to sneak a little extra. But what neither one of you knows is that life doesn't work that way."

Seeing Ginny's curious expression, she continued, "You see, you have to come of age when it's your time. If you try to rush it or put it off, it only gets you into trouble."

"Don't I know it," Ginny mumbled.

"And you can't turn around one day and say 'I'm a big person now.' It doesn't work that way, either. You have to go through all the motions. You have to have all the kid experiences and all the teenage experiences before you can become an adult. Of course, it's not unknown to skip a few, as Darlene has done, but just because she has a baby and will soon have a husband doesn't mean she's all grown up.

"But she'll do it," Laurel said emphatically. "She loves that baby and she's a fighter. But it's not going to be easy."

Laurel stared out through the moon-shadowed trees contemplating the obstacles that could potentially hinder Darlene's path, of which her immaturity was only one. It would, in all probability, be a hard road for the young couple and their ready-made family.

"Laurel?"

Ginny's voice brought her back to the present.

"I know that, up to this point, I haven't been all that I could be. But I want you to know that that's all going to change."

Hiding her surprise, Laurel tried to anticipate what Ginny was going to say next.

"Wanting me to go to college is something that you've made very plain."

Laurel had trouble holding back her smile of victory.

"But," Ginny continued, "my *not* wanting to go has also been clear from the start, hasn't it?"

Her cheek muscles relaxing, Laurel swallowed. "Yes, it has," she said, leery of her sister's tone.

"I'm going to make some changes," Ginny said boldly, "but you need to understand that my attitude about college isn't going to be one of them."

When Laurel opened her mouth, Ginny raised her hand, arresting the argument before it was started.

"Why should I spend four years in college when I have a career at home waiting for me? I don't expect to waltz right in and take over, but you have to admit, I do have some experience. I know how to sell, I know how to count money, right? Well, that's a start, isn't it?

"I want to learn the rest, too. I want to know how to take inventory, how to order merchandise, how to keep the books, calculate insurance, make work schedules, fill out payroll, *everything*." Ginny's gaze was steady as she added, "I want to learn."

Laurel's hopes of Ginny's college education started to tumble, then nose-dived, until they hit rock bottom. Ginny didn't want to go to college. She had made that clear enough, had been saying it loudly all along. But now she was making some definite decisions about what she *did* want, and that was something that was both brand new and pleasantly surprising.

Well, Laurel thought, wasn't that part of the growing process? Making choices and living with those choices?

"I understand."

"You do?" Ginny's voice was dubious.

"Yes, I do. And I'll teach you everything I know about the store." She took hold of Ginny's hand, her words low and somber. "I want you to know that I'll be there with you every step of the way."

So, college was out. Well, at least Ginny was back on track. If not on the right road, at least she was headed in the right direction. Then why was it, Laurel wondered, that Ginny didn't look that happy?

~ ~ ~

The bright lights of the emergency room did nothing to keep Laurel's heavy eyes from drooping. She almost felt as though she were the one, rather than Darlene, who had just given birth. Chuckling to herself, Laurel chalked up her fatigue to emotional stress. It was a lot of work supporting a woman in labor. Every new father who had ever done would surely agree.

Slowly drawing her eyes open, she saw Michael talking to a doctor at the admissions desk. She stifled a yawn and went over to join them.

"She's in great shape," the doctor said. "You did fine."

"How about the baby?" Laurel asked.

"Healthy as can be. His tummy's full and he's all tucked in for the night. Darlene is, too." Then the old man's eyes lit with a teasing glint as he asked, "What in the world were you all doing out on the old valley road while Darlene was in labor?"

"Don't ask," Michael advised gruffly. He took Laurel by the elbow, steering her back over to the empty waiting area.

"We did a good job," Laurel said.

"The doctor seemed to think so." Glancing about him, he asked, "Where's Ginny? I'll take you two home."

"She went in to say good-night to Darlene and the baby. She won't be long."

They sat down on the worn vinyl-covered chairs.

"I called the service station. They're going to tow your car in in the morning and someone will drive it over to you as soon as it's fixed."

"Thanks," she said.

"And I told them not to bring the car back to you unless it had a new tire on the front and a new spare in the trunk," he said gruffly. "I can't tell you how angry I was when I found out they let you drive off without a spare."

Holding his gaze was impossible. Leaving that service station without a spare tire had been monumentally stupid. "Things turned out okay."

"It's incredible that we didn't face a huge tragedy." He shook his head in wonder.

"You look tired," she remarked, wanting desperately to change the subject.

"So do you. I guess all this nervous tension has taken its toll on both of us."

Rubbing his hand over his face, he got up and paced to the window. He stared out for several seconds, his hands stuffed into his pockets, before returning to Laurel's side.

"I've been thinking about you all night." He sat down on the edge of the seat. "You and this situation we've gotten ourselves into. I'm not going to be able to rest until it's out." He leaned forward and placed his elbow on his knee, cupping his chin in the palm of his hand. His eyes, dark with questions, bore into her.

She, too, had thought about him while she'd waited in the darkness of the car for him to return. Reliving the times she'd spent with him, she'd found herself smiling. He'd made her happy; of that she was sure. Even when they'd been forced to act for Ginny, being with Michael had been fun. When they were together she felt whole and happy—as though everything was right in the world.

She loved him. And she'd come to the conclusion that a commitment wasn't important.

Taking what happiness she could, she had decided, was what she wanted.

Sure, she would miss him when she returned home. Her heart would break to leave these beautiful mountains, this wonderful man. But being with him *now* was what she wanted...was what mattered. She'd learn to live with the pain and loneliness later.

"I want you."

The warmth in his tone caressed her, and her heart swelled with tenderness.

These were the same words he'd said to her earlier, and they sounded just as delicious to her now as they had then.

"I want you, too." She was surprised by how quickly she was filled with yearning. "But there's not much we can do about it here."

His gaze dropped to her lips before returning to drink in the hunger he saw in her eyes. Desire pulled them closer like a powerful magnet.

"I don't think you understand." His voice cracked in its huskiness.

"I understand perfectly," she whispered, kissing him on the jaw.

He groaned, a low rumbling in the back of his throat that only she heard. Closing the small gap between them, he pulled her to him.

His kiss was hard, greedy, and she welcomed it. He drank of her sweetness like a man dying of thirst.

He eased the pressure of their kiss to whisper against her lips, "What I meant—"

"Gee, guys!" Ginny's voice held a hint of

laughter. "I can't think of a less romantic place to make out than an emergency center."

Laurel sat up straight, and Michael reluctantly released his hold.

"Is Darlene asleep?" Michael asked.

"Like a baby."

"And the baby?"

"He's sleeping, too, with his fist stuffed in his mouth." Ginny's eyes misted. "He is gorgeous."

Laurel couldn't help but smile thinking of the new baby she'd watched come into the world.

"Darlene wants us to call home, tell Jim he's a daddy."

"That's a good idea." Laurel nodded.

"Well," Michael said, standing to fish into his pocket for the keys, "let's go home and call Jim. Then we can all get some well-deserved sleep."

Chapter Nine

Back at the cabin, Laurel sat on the edge of the couch, feeling none of the welcoming coziness the room usually gave her. The ride home seemed to have taken several hours instead of the short time it actually took. Questions rolled through her mind, one after another, until she thought she'd scream.

Was she sure that sharing a few precious days of unbridled loving with Michael was what she wanted? And even if it was, could she turn her back on everything she believed in—her whole way of life? She loved Michael. She wanted him. And she knew that he wanted her. But would having him for such a short time be worth the hurt and loneliness she'd feel when she returned home? Looking across the room, she saw him standing by the hearth, studying the fire. She was absently aware of Ginny's excited phone conversation with Jim.

Laurel rubbed the palms of her hands together in agitation. Would letting herself go be worth it? Not only that, but could she possibly spend those few wonderful days loving him without showing him her true feelings?

Michael sat down on the hearth and stared unseeing at the hardwood floor. He'd almost told her, had almost gotten it out. He shook his head. Was she ready to hear how he really felt about her? He doubted it. Seriously. What he needed was more time. He needed more time to show her that he hated playing this stupid game, that, in fact, he wasn't playing at all.

He had tried, really tried, to help Laurel out with her problem with Ginny without becoming involved. But all his good intentions had been smashed on their very first date without Ginny.

Thinking back on the night he'd taken her to work with him, he remembered how the firelight had turned her hair to burnished copper, and how she'd laughed when he'd held his marshmallow too close to the fire and scorched it. He had enjoyed being with her. It had been torture to do his job that night, seeing to the campers' comfort, keeping everyone happy, when his eyes kept being drawn to her beautiful face.

He remembered how his heart had warmed when she'd invited two little girls to play a game of ring-around-the-rosy so their parents could enjoy a quiet stroll under the stars. But he also remembered the ugly feeling that had welled up inside him when that guy, innocent for all Michael knew, had sat down next to her. Michael had recognized the feeling instantly. Jealousy. A jealousy so strong that it had surprised him. At that very moment he had known that not only did he want Laurel, he loved her.

But because they were playing this "game" for Ginny's benefit, he'd felt it unwise to tell Laurel of his feelings. So he'd opted to show her instead. With quiet dinners and long walks taken hand in hand, caresses and unexpected kisses when there was no need to act

—these were the things he'd used in an attempt to reveal to her how he felt.

Maybe the intensity of his desire for her was getting in the way of his own judgment, but even after spending so much time with her for the past two weeks, he suspected that she was still unaware of the magnitude of his emotions. Sometimes she responded to him with such passion that it took his breath away. But then, other times, she would pull back. And it was that withdrawal that kept him guessing. The frustration of wanting to be frank and open with her about how he felt had built inside him until it had become an unbearable burden.

He'd probably been stupid to blurt out as much of his feelings as he had tonight at the hospital, but their time was so short and he didn't want to lose her.

But what if she didn't feel the same? His hands clenched into fists at the thought. She wanted him; he knew that. He could and had stirred her desire. But what he wanted was more than physical. It might sound crazy, having known her for less than two weeks, but he wanted her for a lifetime.

"Michael." Ginny's voice broke into his thoughts and he watched her set the phone receiver on the table. "Jim wants to talk to you."

Bounding across the room, Ginny plopped herself on the sofa next to Laurel.

"Jim wants us to stay a while longer so we can bring Darlene and the baby home with us when we go."

"Stay?" Laurel's insides fluttered at the

thought. She didn't know if it was from excitement or dread.

"Yeah. Just long enough for Darlene and the baby to travel comfortably. And he said Mom wants to talk to you, too."

"Mom?" Laurel's back straightened as she jerked to attention. "Is something wrong?"

"I'm not sure," Ginny said. "I don't think so."

Laurel eyed the telephone anxiously. What could be wrong at home? Had her father gone back on his word and left her mother alone? Michael's expression changed, and Laurel knew her mother was on the line.

"Yes, Mrs. Morgan," he said. "They're just fine. We're having a great time together. Yes. Of course. I'd like that very much."

Laurel wished she could hear both sides of the conversation.

"Although your oldest daughter may have something to say about that."

What could they be discussing? Laurel wondered.

"I've been showing them around," he said. "There's plenty more for them to see."

Michael called to her with his eyes, and Laurel stood and went over to him.

"She's right here," she heard him say.

He handed her the receiver and smiled. "It's your mother."

"Thanks." Why did he look like the cat that had swallowed the canary? She lifted the phone to her ear. "Mom?"

"Laurel. Hello, dear."

Laurel barely recognized the energetic voice.

"Mom, is everything okay?"

"Things are wonderful, Laurel. Just wonderful. They couldn't be better. Well, maybe they could." Her voice dropped to a conspiratorial whisper. "Laurel, I'd really like for you and Ginny to stay there a while longer. I realize that Jim has—"

"What?" Laurel wasn't in the habit of interrupting others, but she was that taken aback by her mother's demeanor.

"Just a little longer, dear."

"Mom, what's wrong? Why are you whispering?"

"Nothing's wrong, Laurel." Her mother's tone held a touch of indignation.

"Mom—"

"Laurel, will you listen to me?"

It had been a long, long time since her mom had spoken to her so sharply.

"Your father and I...we've been talking. We've been spending time together, enjoying each other. It's as though we've started over. Please, Laurel, give me a little more time alone with him."

Laurel was so surprised she was speechless.

"Your dad is planning something wonderful for Ginny, too. He's opening a small branch shop and he wants her to manage it. She'll love it, don't you think?"

Again, Laurel couldn't find the words to answer.

"She'll have something of her very own. It's going to be right on the boardwalk. Laurel?"

"I'm here, Mom. I don't know what to say. You sound so...so..."

"Happy?" her mother provided.

Laurel swallowed. *Different* was the word that floated through her mind. *Amazingly different.*

"Yes," she said. "I guess that's it."

"Don't sound so upset." An underlying mirth made the words sparkle.

Tears of joy filled Laurel's eyes. "No...it's just...I'm..."

"You tell Gin what's waiting for her here. And tell her I love her."

"I will. I love you, Mom—Dad, too." Laurel could barely get the words out.

"I love you, too. And, Laurel, that young man I spoke to—he seems very nice."

"He is," Laurel said vaguely, preoccupied by the miraculous change in her mother.

"Bye, sweetheart. I'll see you in a couple of weeks." Laurel stared at the dead phone in her hand. The whole conversation had been incredible. Her mother had said that she loved her. Laurel had known forever that her mother loved her—she had never doubted it for a minute—but it had been years since she'd actually heard the words out loud.

What was that last thing her mom had said? *"I'll see you in a couple of weeks."* The statement brought her up short. Two more weeks? She looked across the room at Michael, whose dark eyes were waiting, glinting with some hidden pleasure.

How could she possibly survive for another couple of weeks without succumbing to the feelings she had for him? A couple of days, maybe. But never for two full weeks! She was sure to make a fool of herself, just as she had when she'd first met him. The thought of those first disastrous meetings with Michael sent a pang of embarrassment through her. Over and over, she'd looked like a blubbering idiot.

She couldn't go through that again. From where she stood she saw two options. She could stay and ultimately give in to the powerful feelings she had for Michael, or she could cut and run. Even an idiot could realize that only one of those options was viable. One option that is, if she wanted to be left with any amount of self- respect. She couldn't make a fool of herself. She had to leave. She had to get away from him.

Placing the receiver into its cradle, she walked slowly, calmly, over to where her sister and Michael sat. She used each methodical step to plan the best way to deliver her news.

"Isn't it great?" Ginny said when Laurel reached the sofa. "Michael told me that Mom sounds fantastic. She wants us to stay out here for two more weeks."

Laurel avoided Michael's eyes. She sat down next to Ginny and plastered a bright smile on her face.

"Dad has a wonderful surprise for you."

"For me?"

Laurel knew Ginny's thoughts about staying were forgotten as her expression took on an air of excited expectation.

"Yes," Laurel said. "And we have to go home right away." She sensed rather than saw Michael go utterly still. She ignored him, wanting to keep Ginny's excitement high. "You're going to have a store of your own. Right on the boardwalk."

"You mean...to manage...on my own?"

"Uh-uh. All on your own."

Ginny squealed and hugged Laurel to her. "A store of my own! I can't believe it." She sat back and looked at Laurel, her smile fading. "But I don't know how to manage a store." She gazed across the room, a faraway look in her eyes. "I've stocked shelves and managed the till. But...but..." She looked back at Laurel, panic written on her face. "Laurel, I'm going to need some help. I don't know the first thing about keeping the books. I've never hired staff. I've never... Oh, Laurel, what if I fail?"

Laurel smiled. "Don't worry. You'll learn everything eventually. And it'll be easier than you think." Looking at the eager flush that warmed Ginny's cheeks, Laurel couldn't help but know that this was the perfect answer to Ginny's problems. Her parents had come up with the ideal solution. Giving Ginny a purpose was like handing her the key to a locked door, a door that led to responsibility and maturity.

Michael sat straight and tense, watching the scene unfold before him. Laurel purposefully avoided eye contact with him. Why was she not telling Ginny the truth? He was certain that Laurel's mother wanted her daughters to extend their vacation. Mrs. Morgan had told him that she needed more time with her husband, and after what Laurel had told him about her mother's condition, he had marveled at this turn of events. He'd also felt as though he'd been handed a reprieve. With Laurel staying on Spring Mountain at least two more weeks; he would have the time he needed to show her how he felt. But here she was telling Ginny they had to leave immediately. Well, he refused to let her bolt like a skittish doe.

Clearing his throat to get their attention, he said, "Laurel, your mother explicitly told me that she'd like you and Ginny to stay. I assured her there were plenty of sights you haven't seen."

Laurel refused to look at him. She knew to meet his gaze would be her downfall. She wanted him so badly she couldn't stand it. But she couldn't have him and not bare her soul. She wanted something more than merely a vacation fling. And that was impossible. He lived and worked in the mountains of Western Maryland. She lived and worked hundreds of miles away on the seashore. It was too complicated. She had to leave here because she couldn't bring herself to take only a part of him and not reach out for the whole.

"Michael told me that Mom and Dad are talking." Ginny's voice was lowered in awe. She took Laurel's hand. "As excited as I am about having my own shop, I think we should stay. Laurel, if they need more time together, we should give it to them." Ginny looked at Michael. "It's okay if we stay in Jim's cabin, isn't it?"

"Sure." He turned to Laurel. "We've had fun so far, Laurel. I'd like you to stay."

She sucked in her breath. Is that what he thought? Was that what he wanted? More *fun*?

Jerking around to face him, she felt a knot rise in her throat. She needed to look at him, wanted to see the man he really was.

She'd meant nothing to him. Nothing! All the time she'd spent learning to care for him, falling in love with him, had only added up to "fun" in his mind.

"You want me to stay?" The words sounded raspy and harsh even to her own ears.

Ginny must have felt the sudden burst of tension because she tugged her hand from Laurel's tight grasp, stood and said with false brightness, "Well, this has been a long day for me. I'm going to bed."

Both Michael and Laurel kept their fixed stare as Ginny left the room. The hurt welled in Laurel's throat until she was sure it would suffocate. As she watched him sitting there, silent and expectant, her wounded feelings slowly turned to anger.

"I asked you a question," Laurel said, her jaw so tight she could barely get the words out.

He took a deep breath. "I heard you. And the answer is yes." He pressed his lips together, pausing a moment before adding, "But you knew that already."

His eyes darkened with desire, and the knowledge that that was all he wanted from her pierced through her heart.

Laurel stood and glared at him. Then she went over to the front door, turned the handle and pulled it open.

Turning back to Michael, she said, "Thank you for all of your help. I do appreciate everything that you've done for me. For Ginny. But I want you to know, Michael, that the play is over. The curtain's been drawn."

The desire that had been evident on Michael's face slowly morphed from bewilderment, to irritation, to anger as he stood and walked toward her. When he reached her, he locked one hand around her upper arm and pulled her out onto the porch, closing the heavy door behind him. He towered over her, ire pulsing in the muscles of his jaw.

"I can't believe you feel that way. I don't believe it."

Laurel pried her arm out of his grip and took a backward step. She kept her voice quiet and controlled. "Well, you better believe it. I'm finished playing. I'm going home. I'm going home as fast as my little legs will carry me."

He heaved a deep, frustrated sigh. Why was she so set on leaving? He walked to the steps and stared up at the stars, rubbing one hand back and forth across his jaw as he dealt with chaos swirling in his chest.

"What about your parents?" he said quietly. "Forget about us for now, us and the game we've been playing. You're mother made a request. Surely you want to give her the time she's asked for." He glanced at her over his shoulder, stuffing his hand deep into his pocket.

Laurel stood there, her lips pressed tightly together. Of course, her parents needed time, and she wanted to give it to them but she couldn't stay here. She couldn't!

"For God's sake, Laurel, your mother is trying

to turn her life around. You've got to give her a little space to do it."

"I'll go someplace else," she whispered. "Ginny and I can pack up the car and go someplace—"

"You're running from me. From what we've enjoyed together," he said. He strode toward her, not stopping until he was inches from her face. "What happened to all your big talk about maturity, Laurel? What happened to—" He cut off the rest of his sentence, his head shaking in clear disgust. "You don't have to run from me."

He exhaled, closed his eyes and dragged his fingers through his hair. "Look, if you're not ready to deal with reality, that's fine with me. You and Ginny can use the cabin as long as you like. You won't see me. I won't come around. You won't even know I live on the same mountain."

He turned then and walked down the steps. Laurel directed her gaze at the thick stand of trees, not wanting to watch him leave. She listened as the truck's door opened and closed, the engine revved and the tires crunched on the gravel as he drove out of her life.

Engulfed by empty silence, she glanced over her shoulder. The empty lane, engulfed by the chilly black night, mirrored her perception of what life would be like for her now. She had succeeded on putting an end to any chance that she and Michael would spend any of her remaining vacation time together. She eased herself down on the porch rocker and looked out into the dark forest, tears slipping unchecked down her cheeks.

"Why couldn't you understand?" she

whispered. "Satisfying the wanting isn't enough without the loving. I couldn't give you just a piece of me. It was all or nothing."

Chapter Ten

Winded from her trek up the steep mountain trail, Laurel stopped to catch her breath. The valley looked as colorful as a vibrant abstract painting, and blue-gray clouds billowed high in the sky above. She remembered Michael telling her that when the "blue smoke" rolled in, snow was sure to follow.

She shivered, not knowing whether her shaking was caused by thoughts of snow or the fact that merely thinking Michael's name brought his face, sharp and clear, to her mind. Defiantly pushing his image aside, she zipped up her jacket and continued her hike.

She crossed the meadow at the top of the mountain and was standing under the huge, lone oak tree before she realized that she'd arrived at the spot where she and Michael had shared their picnic.

What had brought her here? She had purposefully avoided all the places they had visited together—until today. Today every place she went to brought thoughts of him. Was her subconscious deliberately leading her along a poignant path?

It had been five long, empty days since she and Michael had so unpleasantly parted. She'd spent most of them tramping through the forests, trying to keep herself busy, trying to think of anything but Michael.

However, she'd found it impossible. The harder she tried not to think of him, the more he filled her thoughts.

The nights were even worse. Endless, sleepless nights spent staring at the moon through the window. What little sleep she did get was riddled with horrible, gut-wrenching dreams, dreams of Michael coming to her only to tender a scathing laugh and turn away, leaving her alone to fret and pine and wait for him again.

She looked up through the branches of the huge tree and wished she could shed these thoughts of Michael as easily as the oak sloughed off its leaves each autumn. Lowering herself to the ground, she leaned against the rough bark and sighed. A tear slid down her face and dropped onto the back of her hand.

"Stop it!" she muttered, dashing the moisture away. "It's over. It's all *over*."

In the days since he'd said goodbye, Michael had been true to his word. Laurel hadn't seen hide or hair of him. Not that she was hoping to—in fact, she'd been relieved not to have to face him.

She couldn't get things straight in her mind. She thought that knowing Michael wanted her purely on a physical basis would diminish her desire for him, but her feelings were just as strong as ever.

"This is crazy!" she shouted at the top of her lungs. Two blackbirds bolted from the branches overhead. She sat still as her words were carried away by the greedy breeze.

I can't do this anymore, she thought. *This is*

absolute torture. I'll go insane if I stay in these mountains a moment longer.

She closed her eyes and tried to think of home. Ocean City. The shops, the crowds of vacationers, the beach, the dunes, the seagulls. Everything she knew so well. But her thoughts kept turning back to the lush woods, the gurgling streams, the wildflowers, the critters, the craggy cliffs, the awe-inspiring beauty of Maryland's mountains.

In a little over a week she'd be returning to the city, and she was uneasy about what she might find. Things would certainly be different. With Jim managing the old store and Ginny having her own shop, her father at home and her mother happy to have him there, Laurel couldn't help wondering where she would fit in. Oh, she was sure they wouldn't shut her out; she'd been the center of everyone's world for far too long. But things wouldn't be the same. *She* wasn't the same. And neither was anyone else.

What was she going to do with herself? In the past she'd filled so many voids for her family; parent for Ginny, caretaker for her mother, business manager at the shop for her father. But those holes seemed to be growing smaller and smaller, and she was left doubting where that left her. Dragging in a lungful of the cool mountain air, she felt a tremendous longing to stay in this wild, wonderful place, to see what the winter did to this mountain paradise. These hills would look magnificent coated by crystalline snow.

Stop! She shook her head, erasing the picture. Home was where she belonged. She had to return to the place where she used to be needed.

I'm going to cry again, she thought incredulously. She never cried. She'd always been the strong one. She needed something, *anything*, to divert her attention from all this sadness. Taking another deep breath, she stood and brushed off the back of her trousers. She'd go find Ginny. Then they'd pick up a pizza and have dinner with Darlene and the baby.

Darlene's newborn son had a way of making everything seem bright and cheerful.

Her decision made, she started walking briskly toward the cabin.

~ ~ ~

"Laurel, why won't you talk about it? Why do you keep changing the subject?" Ginny's questions hung in the air, tense and awkward. "You're dancing around like your life depended on it."

The three of them, Laurel, Ginny and Darlene, sat sharing a pizza smothered with every topping the small take-out shop had to offer.

Laurel lowered the slice she was about to take a bite of and stared at her sister. "I don't know what you mean. I haven't moved from this spot since I arrived."

Ginny just glared in response.

Finally, Laurel signed. "What is it you want me to talk about?" she challenged.

"You know exactly what I want to talk about," Ginny said. "Michael." She wiped her mouth with a paper napkin. "And you."

"There's nothing to discuss, Gin." Laurel used a tone that would normally convey "Leave it alone," but Ginny wouldn't be put off.

"Give me a break."

"Yeah, give us a break," Darlene chimed in. "We're all family here, right? So tell us what happened."

Ginny jumped in again. "You've moped around here for days. Half the time you've had tears in your eyes. The other half you look like you're sleepwalking."

"I think I'll go check on the baby." Laurel started to rise but was thwarted as both Ginny and Darlene reached out to hold her arms, guiding her gently back down to her seat.

"The baby's fine," Darlene said.

"His belly's full and he's sleeping like a log. So," Ginny coaxed, taking another slice of pizza from the box, "tell us."

"Yes, tell us." Darlene slid back on the couch, ready to listen.

Laurel looked from one to the other. "You guys are ganging up on me, and I don't like it very much."

"We decided that it was the only way we could get you to spill it," Ginny explained.

"There's nothing to tell—"

"There is something to tell," Darlene interrupted. "You've been miserable and we know it has something to do with my almost cousin-in-law."

"Michael?" Laurel's voice was sharp. "What's he said to you?"

"Nothing." Ginny shook her head, thoroughly disgusted. "We can't get him to talk, either. You two were inseparable ever since we got here. Then all of a sudden you're not even speaking to each other. And here I was sure you guys were getting serious. So? What happened?"

Laurel's gaze passed from Ginny to Darlene and back to Ginny. What harm could it do to tell them the truth? she wondered. With all hope of Ginny attending college gone, what did it matter if Laurel fessed up to what she'd done? Besides, talking about it might make her feel better, might help her to sort things out in her own head.

"It was all a game," Laurel blurted out.

Several seconds ticked by.

"A game?" Ginny asked. "What do you mean?"

"Our dating. It never meant anything. It was a game. An act. Michael and I were only acting."

Ginny and Darlene exchanged looks of incredulity.

"But why?" Ginny looked totally confused.

"For you, Gin. For you. And because of that stupid bet we made." Laurel could see from her sister's face that this was going to take a lot of explaining. "You see, it was important to me that you had some other choice besides being forced into working at the shop like I was. I wanted you to go to college—"

"But I want to work in the shop," Ginny said. "I always have."

"I understand that now. I didn't then." Laurel slid to the edge of her chair. "Remember how you said you thought that being responsible would be tedious? Well, Michael agreed to help me show you that responsible people can have just as good a time as the next guy."

194

Ginny just sat there shaking her head, her eyes wide. "Laurel! What a dumb thing to do!"

Falling back against the cushion, Laurel confessed miserably, "It does sound completely stupid when you say it out loud, doesn't it?"

"Yeah. It sure does," Ginny said, her mouth quirking. She and Darlene fell into a fit of giggles.

Laurel sat up and glared at them. "Well, let me tell you, it sounded perfectly reasonable at the time. Even Michael thought so."

"Jeez, Laurel, how did you talk Michael into doing something so lame?" Ginny squeaked.

"You must have done some really good fast-talking to persuade him," Darlene added.

"I didn't have to persuade him to do anything." Laurel's statement was filled to the brim with indignity. "It was his idea."

"His idea?" The question echoed from both girls, and the laughing suddenly stopped.

"Yes. His idea."

"Wow!" Darlene said, astonished.

"Anyway," Laurel continued, wanting to get it over with, "we ended up really enjoying our time together. And even though I never meant to...I mean...even though I never wanted to...I...I've..."

"You fell in love with him," Ginny finished for her. "I knew it! Didn't I tell you that you were in love with him?"

At first, all Laurel could do was nod. Then she shook her head and admitted, "Yeah, well, you knew it before I did, smarty."

"So, what's the problem?" Darlene asked simply.

"The problem is that even though the whole thing turned into something meaningful to me, it didn't to Michael." Laurel tucked her bottom lip between her teeth for a moment before adding, "For him it started out as a game and it ended as a game." Then she shook her head and mumbled, "A game he really didn't want to stop playing."

"So, does he know?" Ginny asked.

"Does he know what?" Laurel threw her napkin into the empty pizza box.

"How you feel about him!"

"Of course not! How could I tell him? He would laugh in my face if he knew I'd fallen for him." Laurel's throat constricted and the tears that welled up again stung her eyes.

"Laurel, I know Michael," Darlene said softly. "I've known him all my life. He's not like that. He wouldn't laugh at you. And he wouldn't go on playing some kind of game, no matter how silly it was, if there wasn't something more to it."

"And the whole thing was his idea," Ginny added. "That says something right there."

"I saw the way he looked at you the night Jimmy was born." Darlene smiled wryly. "I may have been busy, but I still noticed."

"And those kisses I saw!" Ginny smiled and raised her brows. "Laurel, nobody's *that* good an actor."

Laurel looked down at her tightly clenched hands. Could they be right? Could Michael really care about her? Thinking back over their times together, Laurel remembered the caresses and the kisses and the loving endearments Michael had bestowed on her, even when Ginny was nowhere near them. She had thought at the time it was only because he was enjoying himself, having a good time. But Darlene was right about Michael, Laurel thought. He wasn't the kind of person who would take advantage of anyone.

"I think you should tell him," Ginny called out.

"Me, too," Darlene agreed. "What have you got to lose?"

Should she tell him? Laurel mulled it over. What *did* she have to lose?

Ginny stared at her intently. "I'd say you have more to lose if you don't tell him."

Her stomach began to churn with anxiety. No, it was excitement. They might be right! If there was a sliver of a chance that he might have feelings for her, she'd be foolish not to go for it.

"You're right," she exclaimed. "You're absolutely right. I have nothing to lose and everything to gain. I need to tell him." She stood and turned toward the door, then stopped short and turned back. "But I don't know where he is."

"Call him," Darlene offered.

"No." Laurel stood up. "I want to see him. Face to face."

"Let's see," Ginny said, looking at her watch. "It's half past one."

"He'll be working," Darlene said. "Try the ranger station."

Second thoughts seeped into Laurel's brain. "Maybe I should wait till he's finished work."

"Don't wait," Darlene said emphatically.

"Go now!" Ginny ordered.

Laurel grabbed her purse and keys and stormed out the door, leaving Darlene and Ginny grinning like two idiots.

~ ~ ~

Laurel pushed her thumbnail against the pin nestled inside the air intake stem of the tire until all the air hissed out.

I can't believe I'm doing this, she thought for the thousandth time. How can a sane, rational person do something so rash? *He's going to think I'm nuts. A raving lunatic!* As she'd driven by the ranger station and seen Michael's truck there, a crazy plan had taken shape in her mind. She might be uncertain as to how Michael felt about her, but she was sure he would never refuse a plea for help.

She'd parked the car on the side of the road a few hundred yards beyond the station and let all the air out of the new tire Michael had had put on her car. When the wheel's rim was sitting on the ground, the tire a flabby black blob on the gravel shoulder, she rubbed her index finger against the grimy hubcap and wiped a stripe of dirt down her right cheek, just for effect.

She glanced into the side mirror at her reflection and then back down at the flat tire. Pleased with her job, she stood up and wiped the dirt from her hands onto the rear of her cream-colored slacks.

Purposefully she strode toward the cedar-clad

building, ignoring the concentric waves of tension radiating inside her. She breathed in deeply when she reached the station door, running a hand through her hair.

"Oh, what the hell," she muttered and fluffed her hair in all directions.

She opened the door and was met by a petite blond receptionist whose eyes widened at the sight of her.

"Can I help you?"

Laurel looked down the short hall and saw two offices. The doors of both were open, the lights on.

"I need help," she said loudly, hoping Michael would appear.

"Would you like to sit..."

Her eyes darting back to the receptionist, Laurel frantically shook her head. "No, no, thank you."

A green uniformed figure stepped out of one of the offices and Laurel's heart caught in her throat. But when she turned her eyes on him, her heart sank. The ranger had flaming red hair and a sprinkling of freckles across his nose.

Then the man was joined by another and Laurel's knees nearly buckled. It was Michael! And he'd never looked so good.

"I think this lady needs some help," the receptionist said.

Laurel gave a jerky nod of her head and swallowed, trying to relieve the sudden dryness that had her tongue sticking to the roof of her mouth. She hadn't planned on having an audience. As a matter of fact, she hadn't planned at all! All she'd wanted to do was get Michael alone to talk to him, tell him how she felt, but now she had to go on with her helpless act.

Locking her gaze on Michael's face, she said, "I have a flat tire."

Michael's eyebrows rose.

"On my car," she added, vaguely pointing her thumb over her shoulder.

The knots in her stomach tightened as she waited for his reaction. Oh, God, this was worse than she'd ever expected. What if he embarrassed her right here in front of these people? She held her breath as she watched him lean back against the doorjamb and tuck his hand into his pocket.

"I'm sure you're capable of changing that tire yourself," he said easily.

They both ignored the distressed sound that came from the other ranger.

"Oh, yes, I am," she assured him. "But..." Her mind went momentarily blank. She had never considered the possibility that he might refuse to help her. Indecision, mixed with confusion, built in her chest, rising up in her throat until she could almost taste the panic.

Then she saw it: an impish gleam twinkling in his eyes. He was teasing her! A rush of joyous relief filled her, washing away all her doubts and confusion.

"I need you, Michael."

The teasing glint in his eyes was suddenly gone.

"I don't like being an actress. I've discovered that I have no talent for it. Every time my real emotions start to show, I remember that I'm supposed to be acting, and I have to hide my true feelings." Her words came in such a rush, she hoped he understood what she was trying to say.

She saw that he did. The look they shared was so full of emotion that neither one of them seemed able to move.

"Look, lady," the red-haired ranger said, "I can't help you with your acting lessons, but if it's a tire change you need, I'd be more than happy to give you a hand."

Michael clapped his colleague on the shoulder. "That's all right, Joe. I'll help the lady out."

Laurel watched Michael move toward her, and she slipped into his outstretched arms like a weary traveler finding a safe haven. He held her to him, planting tiny kisses along her jaw before covering her mouth with his.

Joe looked over at the receptionist with raised eyebrows and shook his head in wry amusement. "I have a strong suspicion that this has nothing to do with a flat tire." He jerked his head toward his office. "Let's go have a cup of coffee and give these two a little privacy."

"I'm not much of an actor, either," Michael whispered against Laurel's lips. "I was never acting. It was awful trying to show you how I felt without scaring you away. I knew from the beginning that you were the only one for me, but I thought you couldn't feel the same."

Laurel sighed happily when he kissed her neck.

"I thought I'd lost you," he said. "I thought I'd pushed you too far too fast. I needed more time to let you know how I felt. When your mom told me she wanted you to stay, I thought I'd been given a gift." The air left him in a rush. "But when you were so bent on leaving, I knew you didn't care..."

"I wanted to leave," Laurel confessed, "because I wanted you so badly that I was sure I would make a fool of myself if I spent any more time with you."

He leaned away from her without releasing his hold. "We were both fools. Do you know that?"

"Yes," she said wearily, laying her head against his chest. "I know that now. I'm just glad the acting's over." She nestled against him.

Michael tipped her chin up and brushed the dirty streak from her cheek, his fingers lingering to caress her skin. "You didn't really ruin that new tire, did you?"

Laurel grinned sheepishly. "It's nothing that a little air won't fix."

He threw his head back and laughed, then looked down at her tenderly. "I should have known. I love you, Laurel." His whispered words tickled her neck, even as they sent fire through her veins. Then his mouth covered hers in a kiss filled with endless promise.

A note from the author

I hope you enjoyed Mountain Laurel. I wrote the book after spending several summers in Western Maryland with my husband and children. Those fun-filled vacations left me with wonderful memories of hikes along lush mountain paths, crisp autumn days filled with a kaleidoscope of color—and *s'mores!*

To my great surprise, Mountain Laurel won a finalist spot in an international contest called The Golden Heart sponsored by Romance Writers of America. It's rare that an author's first book receives much recognition, so I was grateful for the accolades. Since publishing this book, I've gone on to make the USA Today Bestsellers List with my romance Reclaim My Heart.

If you found Mountain Laurel entertaining, please consider leaving a short book review. You'll help other readers find me. For more information about me and the books I've written, please visit my website at:

www.DonnaFasano.com

Donna Fasano